DIRK DANGER LOVES LIFE

CHRIS ROTHE

Dirk Danger
Loves Life

Chris Rothe

METRO VANCOUVER   DOMINION of CANADA

Dirk Danger Loves Life

This Trade Paperback published October 2011: ISBN: 978–0–9866424–2–5

First Edition eBook published August 2011, ISBN: 978–0–9866424–3–2

Typeset in Warnock

The "Atomic Fez Publishing" logo and the molecular headgear colophon is designed by, and copyright © 2009, Martin Butterworth of The Creative Partnership Pty, London, UK (www.CreativePartnership.co.uk).

PUBLISHER'S NOTE:
This is a work of fiction. All characters in this publication are fictitious and any resemblance to any real places, or persons — living or dead — is purely coincidental. No pugs were harmed or even mocked during the production of this book.

Printed and bound in Canada by Hignell Book Printing; Winnipeg, Manitoba

ATOMIC FEZ PUBLISHING
3766 Moscrop Street
Burnaby, British Columbia, V5G 2C8, CANADA
WWW.ATOMICFEZ.COM

Library and Archives Canada Cataloguing in Publication entry available upon request

1   3   5   7   9   10   8   6   4   2

DIRK DANGER LOVES LIFE

One

Dead Fish, Dead Weight

"I SUCK AT LIFE."

These were the first words out of my mouth upon waking up on the couch to discover that the fish I kept in a bowl on the coffee table had died in its sleep. Well, I'm not sure if it was sleeping or not, but it would be fair to say it died in *my* sleep. I had never named it and didn't even know what kind of fish it was, but I knew a dead fish when I saw one and what to do to remedy the situation... but that would have to wait.

I surveyed the state of my living room. A collection of mugs and soda cans littered the landscape, most half empty and all emitting a foul smell that I'd sadly grown accustomed to. Pizza boxes made genetic labs of themselves, silently orchestrating the development of new species of bacterium and fungus. An overfull ashtray, mountainous in stature, a dormant and silt covered volcano, was placed next to the fishbowl. I briefly hoped that smoke couldn't have entered in through the water and aided in the death of my poor fish. I suddenly found myself realizing that I hadn't made it to bed last night. Arching my back so that I could slide my hand into my back pocket, I produced my badly squashed packet of cigarettes. A single tube of tobacco had survived last night's ordeal. At least it wasn't broken. I sat up, lit up and considered my options: set about to cleaning this mess of a life I was making for myself, or sit in a bewildered state for a good hour and stare at the dead fish. The fish won out in a matter of seconds.

I'd never really taken the time to give a dead fish a careful examination. It floated in its bowl, not upside down, but sort of on its side. One fin partially stuck out of the water, a deep red appendage that looked a bit like dried blood; that almost black, scabby kind of red. Its eyes bulged out a bit. I've read that human beings upon their death usually register either a smile or an expressionless gaze upon their face. This fish had neither. It appeared anguished and tormented, with its amphibian orbs and gaping maw, teeth bared and angry. I had done wrong by this fish, to be sure.

After finishing my cigarette, I lay on the couch and tried to twist my body into the shape of the fish in the bowl. I hung my fin-arm off the couch, low to the ground but not quite touching and stuck my other fin-arm up a bit, bent at the elbow and hanging in the air as if floating there. I opened my eyes wide and started to make fish motions with my mouth, extending my jaw down but keeping my mouth closed. Then I started making bubbly sounds with my fish lips until I sat up, feeling foolish. Dead fish don't make bubble sounds. I suck at mime.

This was not a good day. The day before, I had been fired from the third job in as many weeks and in celebration, went out and got plastered by myself in some little pub not far from my house. There were sports on the television and stale nuts in front of me and I half giggled to myself the entire evening while I took in as many beers as my motor skills would allow. I think I was there until closing, I'm not sure. I don't remember staggering back to my house, I don't remember passing out on the couch and I don't remember anything adventurous that may have happened to me at any point during the blackout.

It was a big blow. Three jobs in three weeks. That's almost an accomplishment. Alright, I admit it, two were with cause. But not the last one.

The first had been in a restaurant. I was working in the kitchen and was making a chicken salad. I was lost in thought, off in a daze and I dropped a piece of chicken on the floor. Then I put it back on the salad. The kitchen manager caught me and we had it out. I guess he doesn't subscribe to the 'ten second' rule. The second had been a job in late night security. All I had to do was sit at a desk and make sure no one went into the building between the hours of eleven P.M. to seven A.M. Turns out I wasn't ready to handle an all night job. The night I chose to pass out in my chair was also the night some kids decided to put a rock through the window and take nothing more than the television I was supposed to be monitoring security cameras on. How I slept through the window breaking I'll never understand. The worst thing about that one was that it made the news. I narrowly avoided being interviewed by the hot newscaster. The most recent job was at a retail store. I was politely told after three days of work that my attitude needed adjusting and my dress did not apply to their code of attire. They felt it would be best for both myself and the company if I would resign my position.

So here I was, hung over, out of cigarettes and acting like a dead fish. Definitely not the best start to any day, but hey, who knows? Couldn't get any worse, right?

As soon as that thought entered my brain, a fit of coughs erupted from my tar filled lungs.

The need to expel the beer in my system reminded me that the fish would need to be disposed of. Picking up the bowl, I brought it to the bathroom.

As the liquid flowed out of my still quivering body a thought occurred. Finishing up with a flush and a quick, soapy rinse of my hands, I went into the living room and after a quick search, found the fish food under the couch. Back in the bathroom, I poured my nameless friend into the toilet and stood solemnly over the burial chamber, a toothless watering mouth of a thing.

"Fish," I began, "You were a good friend. You didn't talk back, you didn't argue and you didn't judge me. As a result, I killed you. Here is some food to take with you to the afterlife." I sprinkled some of the food into the toilet. "Amen." And then flushed.

The fishbowl went back on top of the coffee table. I found a magic marker and wrote an epitaph:

HERE DOESN'T LIE

FISH

WHO WAS COMMITTED BACK TO THE

SEWERS FROM WHENCE HE CAME

A GOOD AND LOYAL FRIEND

HE SHALL BE MISSED

2009-2009

After writing the epitaph, I gave the marker a good sniff and recapped it. Then it was time to get some more cigarettes.

I was actually surprised to find that I was still wearing my shoes. I was equally surprised to find that I wasn't wearing any socks. A quick search behind the sofa yielded the discovery of my coat. Pulling my would-be fins through the arms of the jacket, I tucked my hair, (which had begun to resemble the lair of a rather insidious spider) beneath a cap and headed out the door.

On the two-and-a-half block walk to the shop where the smokes lay in wait behind a counter guarded by a toll-collecting man with yellowed teeth and thinning hair, I thought about my situation, a situation that I had been trying not to think about for months now. I was on to my second eviction notice. I had unpaid bills piling up. I had a severe lack of cash flow. It seemed I was irresistibly fire-able. The cupboards in my home were nearly empty and I was more content to smoke than to eat. That one I couldn't figure out. And now, on top of all of that, I couldn't even take care of a fish. I'd have cried if there wasn't so much on my mind.

The worst of it all was that I seemed to take everything so off-handedly. I acted as if things would work out for themselves, that all I needed to do was stumble about and before you knew it, I'd be debt free, loving my job and have a beautiful woman who would love me no matter how bad things got.

The store loomed. There it was, open for business and greedily awaiting the opportunity to take what little money I had left.

My coffee and cigarettes came out to eleven dollars and sixty-two cents. I didn't have enough cash for both. I pulled out my debit card and gave it a quick kiss for good luck. Not really having a good idea of just how much I'd spent on booze the night previous, I had a sinking feeling I'd be facing rejection in the near future. There had been around two hundred dollars in my account, but I didn't trust my current bout of drinking with that much money. For all I knew, the whole bar had a round on me last night. I was handed the PIN pad.

The handset asked me if I was being charged the right amount. I told it that I was. *Green button.* It asked me for my account information with a smirk on its face. It knew this was a loaded question. Think man, think! Savings or chequing… savings or… oh, what the hell… SAV *button.* It asked for my PIN, almost nonchalantly, as if it had already beaten me. But this was not over yet, not by a long shot. *o-o-o-7, green button.* And then, those fateful words... *PROCESSING: PLEASE WAIT FOR MESSAGE.* Fingers crossed. Toes crossed. Thumbs... patient. And then:

APPROVED. THANK YOU

"No," I said aloud, wagging my finger at the machine, "thank *you*." It was a small miracle that the entirety of my account had not been sipped, chugged and guzzled away.

The clerk gave me a look. I gave him a look back and snatched up my purchases. There may have been an exchange of parting pleasantries, but I was lost in a wave of emotion, pleased that I could not only drink my coffee, that I could not only smoke my cigarettes, but that I should be lucky enough to do both at the same time.

I leaned up against a telephone pole in the alley leading back to my place. Balancing the coffee in the crook of my elbow, I unwrapped the package of cigarettes as if it was Christmas and they were just what I wanted. The wrapper was lost to the wind as I fumbled for my lighter. Once the first of many had been successfully fired up, I carefully removed the coffee from my elbow and turned to walk home.

Mid-turn, I noticed something on the telephone pole. Something white. Something paper. It was one of those ads with the tear-away phone numbers. On it was the following sentiment:

LOSE WEIGHT NOW!
ASK ME HOW!
555-CHUB

Below this there were several strips of the number listed above. Three spaces where numbers had been removed made the page look like a yokel with missing teeth and a nasty overbite. Looking at the sign I shrugged and considered the page for a moment. I didn't need to lose weight. That was one problem I didn't have; thin as a toothpick from my strict regimen of poison swirled with a light dose of acid.

The phone number certainly stuck out to me. Was it a coincidence? Did this person just happen to have a phone number that contained the word chub or did they buy it for this explicit reason? Can you even buy phone numbers for any particular reason? So many of life's little mysteries eluded me...

Immediately I wanted to call it. I would ask this "Me" how to lose weight. At least it would give me something to do this afternoon in between sitting and staring and staring and sitting.

When I arrived back at my mess I sat and I stared. I stared at the phone number for a moment, and then I laid it on the coffee table next to the monument to my dead pet. A sip of coffee, another lit cigarette. And then I went to find the cordless.

Dial tone... 5-5-5-C-H-U-B... Ring... Ring... Ri—

"Hello?" came the voice that would free me of flab, the mysterious, "Me".

"Hello, is this 'Me'?"

"I suppose. Though if you have to ask, maybe it isn't."

"I'm calling in regards to your sign."

"Which sign was that?"

"The one about losing weight."

"Ah yes."

There was a pause.

"So, how can you help me lose the pounds?"

"You're fat. Stop eating."

Click.

????

Well that wasn't what I had been expecting.

Dial tone... Redial... Beep-boop-boop-beep-boop-beep-beep... Ring...

"Are you still fat?"

"I never was actually."

"I'm a miracle worker."

"That's seriously all you have to offer? You let fat people call you and then you insult them?"

"Yes."

"Why?"

"Sometimes people need to hear the ugly truth."

"What if it's a thyroid thing?"

"Oops."

I was beyond fascinated. Thyroid or no, I kind of liked his philosophy. I had a whim.

"I may not be fat," I began, "but I might stand to hear some ugly truth."

"Hmm. What are your symptoms?"

"I suck at life."

"I see."

"Well?"

"Well what?"

"Can you help me?"

There was another pause. And then, the voice said, "I think I might be of service. But first, I need to know, are you willing to meet with a complete stranger to discuss the details of your situation?"

Maybe it was my carefree attitude, maybe it was a lust for adventure or maybe it was just because I was curious, but without hesitation I said, "Yes. Absolutely."

"Good to hear. When are you available to meet?"

"Let's see... I'll have to check my Day-Timer..."

"No one who has a Day-Timer calls it a Day-Timer. Who are we trying to kid?"

"No one apparently."

"I assume anytime is good for you then?"

"Yeah. I'm wide open."

"Perfect. Then we shall meet."

"When and where. And for that matter, who?"

"I'll meet you at the airport. Gate five at five tomorrow evening. I'll be holding a sign with my name on it."

"And your name is?"

"Dirk Danger."

"Dirk Danger?"

"Dirk Danger."

"Danger?"

"*Dirk* Danger."

"I see."

"See you then, fatty."

Click.

And that was that. I had an appointment with Danger. How exciting.

Two

A Journey Without a Ticket

"D AMN."

I had purchased a lottery ticket in one of the many airport convenience stores, one of those crossword ones, where you have to use the letters you scratch to spell out the words on the board. I had bought it in a desperate attempt to win fifty thousand dollars so I wouldn't have to meet with this guy, this... 'Dirk Danger'. Unfortunately, the only word I managed to spell completely was the word 'Idiot' and they don't pay out on irony. There were a series of second thoughts floating through my head, with third thoughts trailing close behind them and some fourth thoughts gaining mileage fast. How desperate does a person have to be that they will seek help through some unidentified swami, I asked myself.

I pocketed the key I had used to scratch the worthless piece of cardboard and threw the ticket in the trash. I always used a key to scratch lotto tickets. I liked the idea of winning the lottery and taking that key to a framing store. I'd get a ridiculously gaudy wooden frame, inlaid with vines or waves, or vines *and* waves; maybe a nice set of dismembered peacock feathers... something like that. The gaudy frame would hold within a nice red velvet panel, and on that velvet panel would rest the lucky key. I would frame it in my living room and host big parties, affluent affairs with all sorts of debonair types, holding their fancy *hors d'œuvres* in one hand and a glass of fine *Champagne* in the other. I would schmooze with the crowd and inevitably one of these snobby sorts would ask me, "Sir, what *is* the key to your success?" and I would point to my key and say, "That right there, my friend, is the key to my success." At this point we would laugh heartily and enjoy the festivities.

Now that's fantasy for you.

The airport was, as usual, buzzing with activity; every kind of person imaginable, most tired and all seemingly in a hurry. I felt like the only one with no reason to be there. It felt more than ever like I was going nowhere.

I made my way to the escalator so as to browse the shops on the second floor, kill some time. It wasn't quite five yet and I was still uneasy about meeting this 'Danger' guy and I needed some the kind of distraction that only airport gift shops can supply. They are always so chock full of memorabilia the likes of which you've never seen. If you don't already own one, a miniature stuffed beaver wearing a Mountie hat and holding a tiny Canadian flag in its furry little paw, is the perfect gift for any friend, relative or co-worker. The beaver will always have a name too, something cute like 'Bucky' or 'Pelty' or... 'Little Mountie McRodent Jr'. Such are the joys of the airport gift shops.

After one or two knick-knack shops I began to become nauseated with the thought of having these horrific trinkets lined up on my coffee table, stuffed along my bookshelf and tucked neatly along my bedspread. Out of one shop and across the hallway to the obligatory airport bookstore. High up on the 'New Fiction' shelf were dozens of copies of *A Million Little Pieces*. With a smirk I headed over to the magazine rack and found a total of no porn, 1 men's magazine which could almost count as porn if you happen to be fifteen, and thousands of *Cosmo*-esque monstrosities that promised to give you YOUR BEST ORGASM EVER... no, seriously... EVER!

Any orgasm is my best orgasm, so I headed on. None of the other books really caught my attention. I sighed, sighed louder and left the bookstore.

No longer wanting to wander I decided to sit and to stare. A bench sat against a wall next to a water fountain. I sat closest to the fountain and took in the people, all of them talking. All the chatter built up in my head. My brain was foggy. I kept wondering why I was actually here. Did I really hate myself enough to reach out to a total stranger for help? Did I really hate myself? The question I kept asking above all else was "Why the hell would anyone call themselves 'Dirk Danger'?"

Through my foggy thoughts, the conversations of the passersby bled into one long collage of words, myriad voices, people yelling, frustrated, missing loved ones on the other side of a cell phone, patient, complacent, all talking, yammering, hammering at my eardrums, melding and colliding...

I miss you so much that I lost my baggage *when this hippie rolls up and tells me to* **TAKE THAT OUT OF YOUR MOUTH GODDAMN IT! No, the plane's delayed** 'cause daddy said I could have a popsicle **but the guy was totally hot, so I did it anyway** AND NOW I DON'T KNOW WHERE I LEFT THE KEYS TO MY BRIEFCASE. Yeah, we'll be there at around three after I get a muffin and a cup of coffee and I just want to strangle someone, fuck! THERE'S NO 'I' IN SEX but there's tea at the other shop so I have to take a powerful whiz about now **and... oh, here's the water fountain!**

Time for a cigarette.

On my way outside, I passed by gate five, and unfortunately, before I had a chance to get to a designated smoking area, there emerged a perfectly normal looking man, with a perfectly normal looking haircut, and some perfectly normal looking clothing, holding a perfectly absurd cardboard sign that read 'DIRK DANGER'.

My smoke would have to wait.

Three

Interrogation and a Light Snack

"SHALL WE TAKE IN a meal?"

Dirk had an odd way of speaking. We'd done our brief introductions, during which he called himself "The Dirk Danger". It wasn't as if he was saying he was "The Dirk Danger". He said it in much the same way you would say "the apple" or "the trampoline".

"I'm not really that hungry," I replied.

"T'is a shame," he said. "Airport food is great! Much better than airplane food." He looked around a bit, accentuating the movement of his head so that he looked like a hose whipping about under too much water pressure. "Where's the closest place? I hope you don't mind if we sit down for a bite while we chat. I'm in the mood for food."

I shrugged. "Doesn't matter much to me," I said.

"Excellent. I think I know a good place up the escalator. Follow me!"

Dirk started off at a brisk pace and I had to hurry a bit to catch up with him.

"I must say," said Dirk, "you don't look a thing like I thought you would."

"Oh?" I asked.

"No, no, not a teeny bit. I pictured you as a potbellied laze-about with a three day old growth of beard and a snaggletooth."

"A snaggletooth? Why?"

"I thought it added character."

We boarded the escalator.

He continued: "Instead, I find this ordinary looking guy, dressed like an ordinary looking guy, with no pot belly, no beard growth and, and I must add that I'm disappointed to say, no snaggletooth. Sharp tie by the way."

Ties are a weakness of mine. I think that at one time, I had more ties than I did all other articles of clothing combined.

"Thanks," I said.

"So you suck at life, do you?" asked Danger, stepping off of the escalator.

"Mmmm hmm."

"How so?"

We were approaching a bar and grill. Dirk was just opening the door when I started to reply, but never got a chance to, because the biggest smile I'd ever seen in my life shot through the gaping restaurant doorway and stopped us dead in our tracks. The smile belonged to the hostess of said restaurant, and I wish I could report to you what her other features were like, but even as I looked at her, all I could see was a frightening ear-to-ear grin with a pony tail sticking out the top of it and menus in its hands.

"HI HOW ARE YOU TODAY?" the Smile bellowed.

"Fine thank you, madam. Your finest booth for two, if you may?" Dirk made a slight bow as he spoke.

"SMOKING PREFERENCE?"

"Du Maurier."

There was a slight pause from the bewildered Smile, and a grin from me.

"UH... ?"

Dirk turned to me. "Do you puff the puff?" he asked.

"Yeah," I replied, still grinning.

"Ah. Now that I did expect. Smoking my good madam and the sooner the better! I've got a craving for beef the likes of which you've never seen!"

If ever a smile could look confused, this one certainly managed to pull it off. It motioned for us to follow and sat us down in a small booth on the lounge side.

"JUST TO LET YOU KNOW, OUR DRINK SPECIALS FOR THE DAY ARE..."

"Oh, we won't be drinking," said Dirk.

"ALL RIGHT THEN! I'LL LET YOUR SERVER KNOW YOU'RE HERE! HAVE A GREAT MEAL YOU TWO!" the Smile gave a cute little giggle and hurried off.

"Sorry about that," said Dirk. "You can drink if you'd like. She was creeping me out a little."

"No worries," I said and then, looking back to see if she was still within earshot, said, "me too."

"So life?" asked Dirk.

"Yeah, I suck at it."

"And why exactly is that?"

"The reasons are many."

I paused for a moment, not really sure what to say. The restaurant we were in was terribly gaudy, with traffic signs, neon lights and even a pair of antlers up on the wall. The serving staff was dressed all in black, the men in loose fitting polo shirts and the women in tip improving skin tight Lycra or some such thing.

Dirk pried in again, looking down at the menu as he spoke. "So you suck at life... *why?*"

"Well... I don't know really. Like I said, there's a lot to it."

He put the menu down and leaned closer to me. "I figured you might not want to be too open about the whole life sucking circumstances, so I did us both a favour." He reached into his shirt pocket and pulled out a small notebook. "I've prepared some questions that will hopefully give me insight into who you are and why you do the things you do and why you seem to suck at all of them."

"Uh... what kind of questions?"

"Oh, all sorts. Pick what you're having and we shall begin!"

"I'm really not very hungry," I said, fumbling into my pocket for my cigarettes. There was a pack of matches in the ash tray, which was a bonus because I couldn't seem to find my lighter at the moment. Dirk flipped open his notepad as I whipped out a smoke, snatched the matches and struck the flame to my face. "I think I'll just have coffee."

"Very well then. I shall have a beef sandwich with a side of beef pudding," he looked up at me, expecting to see the curious look that was on my face and explained, "It's what I like to call a beef dip."

"Takes a lot longer to say than beef dip."

"I've found that it's more fun to say things in a drawn out and ridiculous fashion than it is to say them 'straight-laced', as it were. Also, the word 'hodgepodge' should be employed as often as possible."

At least he'd be entertaining.

"So, here comes the questioning!"

"Shoot," I said as I spat out a steady stream of curling smoke.

Dirk brought a pen out from one of his pants pockets and began. "How old are you?"

"24."

"Where do you live?"

"Nowhere soon. I'm about to be evicted from my apartment."

"That sucks," said Dirk.

Our server rolled up. She was nearly too attractive to look at, so, to avoid embarrassment, I didn't.

"Hey boys! How are you today?" she said, her words slathered in server syrup.

"Salty," Dirk said without a pause.

"Would you like some water?"

"Aye," said Dirk. "Water and your beef dip. With some gravy for my skinny potatoes. And my smoking accomplice here will have some coffee."

"Beef dip, one coffee and water," she said. I sneaked a look at her as she bobbed her head from side to side as she jotted the order down. I liked the way her hair moved around her shoulders as she did it, and at the same time thought that her bobbing was singularly annoying. "Anything else for you boys?"

"Nay."

And after whatever pleasantries servers usually dish out at this point, she was gone.

I was nearly done what was certain to be my first of many cigarettes this evening.

"So, where were we?"

"I just told you that I was being evicted," I reminded him.

"Ah, yes, that's right. Well then... let's see..." he tapped his pen against the pad. I butted out, took out another and lighted up. "Where have you always seen yourself living?"

I had to think about that. "I guess I've always liked the idea of living in an apartment," I said. "You know that episode of *The Simpson's* where the school gets all that money from the oil deposit underneath it?"

"The Dirk Danger has little time for television."

"I see. Do you always do that third person thing?"

"No, not really. Only every so often. Why? Does it bug you?"

"A little."

"The Dirk Danger will try and keep it to a minimum."

"Thanks."

I rolled my eyes and continued. "Anyway, there's this episode of the show where the school in Springfield discovers that it's sitting on a huge oil deposit and that therefore, the school is rich. The principal starts asking all of his staff members how they should spend the oil money and the janitor, very single minded-ly, responds that he'd like a solid gold broom. I think it's the same way with my apartment complex."

"Apartment complex! That's a good one."

"I... oh, I see. Pun not intended."

"I'm writing it down as we speak. Sorry, keep going."

"So I've always lived in apartments. Ever since I moved out of my mom's house, I've been going from apartment to apartment. And I think, ideally, I'd like to live in a penthouse apartment, with a pool and some trees on the balcony. I've always wanted a solid gold apartment, so to speak."

"It would be slippery."

"Next question?"

Our drinks arrived and the server left without fanfare.

Taking a sip of water, Dirk resumed his interrogation. "Where do you work?"

"I just got fired for the third time this month," I sighed.

"I'm starting to get a feel for your 'I suck at life' situation. What happened?"

I told him the story, all three stories about my untimely demise from each of my occupations. He chuckled at all three. Next...

"Where have you always wanted to work?"

I didn't have to think about this at all. "Honestly, I've always wanted a nice simple desk job. Even a secretary job would be all right in my book. Guys usually have a hard time becoming receptionists though. The market is still sexist; believe me, I've tried. All I can ever get are those stupid restaurant jobs or those insipid cleaning jobs. I'm just not cut out for it, you know?"

"Mmmm-hmmm. Maybe you're not trying because you aren't getting what you want?"

Exhaling a plume as I spoke: "No, I don't think that's it."

"Moving right along... what did you want to be when you were a kid?"

Again, a no-brainer. "I wanted to be a palaeontologist at first. When I was really young... I think I was five or so."

"Liked dinosaurs, eh?"

"Yeah, I loved them. Then at some point, I figured that all of the dinosaurs would likely be dug up by the time I got old enough to hunt for them, so I gave it up."

"Did you ever decide on a different career path?"

"Yeah, eventually. I was fourteen or so, lying in bed, and suddenly a poem came to me. I'd never written anything before, and suddenly there it was. I felt like I'd actually been visited by an honest to goodness muse. Suddenly there was this poem that I just thought was fantastic, so I raced out of bed, grabbed a pen and a piece of paper and jotted it down. The clincher though, was when I went to school the next day and showed it to my friends. They just loved it and I loved the positive feedback. From that moment on, I wanted to be a writer. Still do."

"You still *want* to write? Do you write or do you just want to?"

"Oh I write every now and then, but I get so down on myself. I write something, leave it for a week, go back to it and think, '*That is absolutely, the worst thing ever written in history*' and then I file it away and don't ever look at it again. I have binders and binders full of unreadable crap."

"I think you should probably be the last one to judge it. Artists are notoriously hard on themselves."

"I'm not letting anyone else read it, are you crazy?"

"Mmmm hmmm..." Dirk muttered, jotting something down.

"What are you writing?"

"Oh, nothing. You'll see. Next question! Are you currently in a relationship?"

I sputtered on my smoke. "Why, you interested?"

"HA! No, sorry. Not into that. Oh, wait, you aren't gay are you? I don't want to offend..."

"No, I'm not gay. And no, I'm not in a relationship. Why, you gonna hook me up?"

"All right, I'd like to get one thing perfectly clear: I am not here to get you laid. I will not even approach the subject of women with you in our time together, should we indeed have time together. I just needed to know if there are any obstacles to me helping you should you decide to accept my help."

"A girlfriend would be an obstacle?"

"Only the Mount Everest of obstacles! I'd have to make sure you two had time together and she'd be indignant that I'd be taking up so much of your free time and on and on and on! I've got nothing against women, or against you having a girlfriend for that matter, I just don't want to share you if it comes to that?"

"I see. What's next?"

"How long ago did you move away from your parents?"

I snorted. "More like 'how long ago did my parents move away from me?'"

"You were abandoned?"

"Not as such, no. My parents divorced when I was seven. I don't really know my father all that well. He left town and other than a phone call here and there, I don't really hear from him all that much. I'm not even sure which city he lives in at the moment. I used to get that information from Mom, but I try not to speak to her too often."

"Why not?"

"Because she never had the time of day for me, you know?"

"No, I don't."

"Well, after my parents split up, there was hardly a custody battle, but there was a fight over my child support money. Mom spent more time trying to get money for me than she did trying to raise me. She was on the phone with Dad at least once a day for the longest time until one day she just gave up. Oh, and the money? Not really for me."

"She spent it?"

"On alcohol and babysitters."

"That's not the best parenting in the world, but it's not the worst either."

"But I don't know anything other than that, and to me, that was the worst. I didn't get beaten every day, or have to watch Mom shoot up heroin or anything, but I was neglected and to me, it's the worst way to grow up. It's perspective."

"Yes, I suppose you're right. You only see through your own experiences..." he trailed off, again scratching pen against paper.

"After she stopped talking to Dad, she was always out in the bar, trying to pick up a 'new Daddy'. So no, I didn't leave them, they left me."

"So you didn't have any brothers or sisters?"

"None that I know of." A smirk on my face and a swig of my cup of bitter, acrid coffee.

"What about friends?"

"What about them?"

"Did you have a lot of friends growing up?"

"Nope. I was always kind of a loner."

"What about now?"

"Do I have any friends?"

Dirk nodded.

"Actually, no... not really, no."

"Seriously? Not a single one?"

"Honestly, I really don't."

"Why not?"

"No one really seems to fit, you know? You meet someone and you go, 'Yeah, they might be a great friend!' but it turns out that they only want money or a place to crash for a while or whatever."

"Maybe you're looking for chums in all the wrong places?"

"Maybe."

"What's your happiest memory?"

I coughed a little. "Kind of a lame question, don't you think?"

"Yes, yes I do. I just wanted to see what you'd come up with."

I thought for a moment. "I'm not really sure..."

"Nothing comes to mind?"

"Well, maybe... hmmm. I suppose when I got my first pet. That was happy... for a bit..."

"A bit?"

"It was a stray cat. It was starving. I was only a kid. I named him Bony."

"Cute."

"I took him in hoping Mom wouldn't know, and for a while, we were the best of friends. I brought him in when I got home from school and we read books together. Well, I read him stories and he purred. I remember once, Mom asked me who I was reading to and I told her I was practicing reading out loud for school. She bought it for a while."

"Then what happened?"

"Mom found out, no more cat. That was that."

"What's your unhappiest moment?"

"Every one but that one."

"Even this one?"

"I'm kind of undecided."

"Well, golly gumdrops, we'll make it swell, I promise!"

"You're an odd guy, Dirk."

"Thank you!"

We paused for a moment, locked in an awkward stare. It was broken by the arrival of Dirk's beef dip.

"So?" I asked.

"Fo wha?" Dirk asked with a mouth full of hot beef sandwich.

"So what's the score? Where do we go from here?"

He swallowed and said, "I have a proposition for you."

"What's your proposition?"

"Well," he said, "if you're being evicted and are currently jobless and quite clearly lost, why don't you come and stay with me for a month until you can get back on your feet? I've already worked out something of a lesson plan, but it's only very preliminary and is subject to change."

"Lesson plan?"

"Yeah! You suck at life, I aim to try and teach you how not to suck at it. What do you say?"

"I say 'I don't even know you that well'! What if you are just trying to lure me into your house so that you can kill me or something?"

"I guess you don't. However, I say things like 'golly gumdrops', so how bad can I possibly be?"

"You have a point."

"Look, I know that the idea is a little strange, but give it a try. Tell you what: we'll make it a month. You stay with me for a month and if by that time you aren't completely satisfied, you can leave and go live on the street? What do you say?"

I don't think that I was thinking clearly. All I was certainly thinking was that I was just about out of luck. No house and no job and no family I cared to run to meant living on the streets for sure, and I didn't want that... not in a million years. And so, thinking clearly or not I said, "All right, fine..."

26

with a sigh and hoped to hell I wouldn't regret it. Dirk smiled and chewed on his beef.

Such an odd fellow...

Four

The Birth of the Cheesebomb

"I CERTAINLY HOPE THAT ISN'T mustard."

Dirk was looking rather disdainfully at a stain on my couch.

"Does it matter? We're leaving the couch anyway, aren't we?"

"Yeah, but, man..."

I sighed. We were cleaning out my apartment. Well, taking what was worth taking, anyway. The way Dirk described it was that we were abandoning my unnecessary flab and was making suggestions as to what we should keep and what we should axe.

"All photos must come with you."

"I don't know if I have any photos..."

"Rubbish. You have photos. What's this box here?"

"No! Don't..."

Dirk let out a low whistle. "Wow... that's a lot of porno. You know we're not bringing this, right?"

I nodded, face red with embarrassment.

"Good. Jesus that's an ass-load of girly mags. I... no, you know what, we are bringing this and then we're burning it. This just ain't right..."

Dirk took the box to the front door *tsk tsk*-ing all the while.

I tried to ignore the embarrassment and focus on the here and now. His comment about the photos had me thinking.

Dirk re-entered the room shaking his hands out in front of him.

"Did you just wash your hands?"

"Why don't you have a towel in that bathroom?"

I rolled my eyes at him and turned back to the boxes.

"Dirk?"

"Yippers?"

"Seriously, I don't have any photos. No pictures of my parents, my friends, no vacation stuff... certainly not any girlfriend photos. I never really realized it before, but it's kind of depressing."

"Well, you have an awful lot of disgusting vagina photos. But then, it's true what they say, no disgusting vagina could ever replace your mother." Dirk put his hand on my shoulder. "Now is not the time for sadness. It's time we finish up. What have we gathered so far?"

"Let's see... all of my clothes, dishes, toiletries... television... music... I think that's it."

"Do you not have anything of sentimental value to you?"

"The fish bowl?" I had shown Dirk the fishbowl epitaph as soon as we had arrived at my apartment. He had wanted to see it.

"You aren't taking that with us. It's a reminder of the time you hit rock bottom. We can't bring it along. It's up from here on in my friend. What about a souvenir from a trip or something?"

I shrugged and shook my head.

"Present from a loved one?"

"Nope. Nothing comes to mind."

"Aha!"

"What?"

"You said that you wanted to be a writer!"

"Yeah?"

"And you mentioned at the airport that you have binders of writing stored away somewhere."

"That was slightly exaggerated. It's actually just *a* binder. It is big though."

"It doesn't matter how big it is or how many of them there are, that certainly has to come! It works nicely into my plans, you adorable little muffin you! Now get that and meet me in the car. We've got porno to burn. Unless of course, you can think of anything else you'd really like to bring with you?"

I thought about it while Dirk took the few things by the door out to the car. I had always kept most of my possessions in boxes and looking at them now I could see why. All of this crap was useless: scraps of paper from high school physics class, old magazines, pieces of Lego and miscellaneous unused cookware. All of my books had been lost during the last move. A very regrettable loss. Nothing on the walls. Not even a *poster*. This was the first time I was noticing the absence of all of these things in my house... in my life. And now here I was about to go bunk with Dirk bloody Danger for a month while he helped me to become a better me. I kept telling myself "The less you think about all of this the better." Easier thought than done.

It took me some digging to find the binder. It was in the bottom of the first box I'd looked in, but I realized that after not finding it and digging through all of the other boxes. There it was, a little zip-up binder containing all of my terrible poems and hackneyed attempts at prose. As bad as it all surely was, I couldn't bear to part with it. I carried the binder to the door, locked up the twist mechanism on the door handle and threw the keys in the middle of the living room before closing the door tight. I tried to forget about the eviction and focus on the fact that I didn't really have to deal with it anymore.

Dirk was waiting in the car, an old family sedan, steel blue and in immaculate condition as if it had just rolled off the lot in 1983.

"Did you find the binder?"

I held it up for him to see as I climbed into the car.

"Excellent. You realize of course that I'll have to peruse it."

"No way!"

"Why not?" Dirk started up the car and we pulled away from where I used to live. A slight pang of guilt washed through my stomach at the thought of the mess we'd left for the landlord.

"Because it's personal! Would you want someone thumbing through your terrible writing? It's embarrassing, it's personal; forget it."

"I wouldn't mind someone thumbing through my anything. And besides, it's probably not as bad as you think it is. Also, I can gain a little more insight into your personality. And see if you have any real talent."

"You want to peek into my secret garden?"

"Hell yeah I do!"

"Weirdo."

We drove in silence for a while.

"So," I asked him, "what kind of lessons do you have planned for me?"

"Haven't given it too much thought yet. Just ideas here and there. I figure I'll work out my game plan this evening while you meet the associates."

"The associates?"

"Yeah, my roomies."

"I thought you lived alone?"

"Why?"

"Just a feeling."

"Do I seem like a loner to you?"

"No, I just figured is all..."

"'Cause I'm not a loner."

"Never said you were."

"I'm having you on! Lighten up." He continued, "Yeah, I live with three other guys. They have stories similar to yours but much worse."

"You really like helping people out don't you?"

"We've all known each other a long time. They aren't really like me at all, and they do their own thing around the house but they aren't drag asses and they are good for a laugh."

"What are their stories?"

"In due time, my good amigo, in due time."

The rest of the drive, Dirk pestered me into finally handing over my binder. I figured it wouldn't really hurt for him to take a look at it.

We pulled up to a good sized house in a nice area of town, not quite suburban but close enough.

"Nice digs, Dirk! Is it yours?"

"Bought and paid for."

"How the hell? What do you do for a living?"

Dirk shrugged. "Let's get your stuff inside."

Letting my curiosity be for the moment, we pulled all of my things into the house. Dirk seemed to enjoy unravelling everything about himself slowly, like a mystery. I could come to enjoy that. Either that or it would quickly annoy the hell out of me.

We piled my stuff near the door and Dirk called out, "Honey, I'm hooooome!" in a disturbing falsetto.

"Yo!" came a reply from somewhere beyond the door.

"The associates are in the house," Dirk said, matter of fact.

"Where do you want this stuff?"

"We'll leave it here for now. The associates all live downstairs and I think the spare room is ready, but I'll have to have a peek in there first. Shall we meet the lads?"

"Sure. Let's go."

Dirk led the way into a very nice living room. The furniture was all black leather; there was a small woodstove off in one corner. Photographs covered the walls. The photographs weren't of people but of objects, all very close up: a single blade of grass in focus while the rest of them blurred in the wind behind them; a piece of wood with scraps of paper, nails and staples sticking out of it; a fraying rope slashing across a slimy green background; odd things. The furniture was arranged in a V shape facing a good sized television and on that furniture sat three guys, all around twenty-fine to thirty and all holding a stem from a large hookah that sat on the coffee table in front of them. The room was a hazy gray.

"Hey, hey, Danger my man! What have you brought us?" one of them asked.

"A new roomie. Well, for a while anyway. I'm helping him out in a jam," Danger responded.

One of them took a big hit, exhaled and said, "Welcome aboard man!"

I wasn't sure what I thought about this. Drugs made me uneasy.

"Allow me to introduce everyone," Dirk announced. "Counter-clockwise, we have Jimmy," he gestured with his hand towards a lanky fellow in a ball cap with a long and pointy nose and a very big grin on his face.

"Pleasure," said Jimmy.

"Likewise," I said.

"This," continued Dirk, moving on to the next guy, "is Robert."

Robert was a chunky fellow with curly black hair and no grin. He nodded at me and I nodded back.

"Lastly, but certainly not leastly, we have Soup."

"Soup?"

"Soup."

"Why Soup... if you don't mind my asking..."

"Because," Dirk hesitantly answered for him, "It's uh, all he usually eats. Fellas, we need a nickname for our new friend here. Try to come up with something by the end of the night." Dirk turned to me. "Hey, why don't you sit down with these guys and have a chat while I figure out our game plan, alright."

"Uh, yeah... sure."

Dirk patted me on the shoulder and said, "There's a good lad."

And with that, he was off, and I was now alone in the room with these strange guys, all of them puffing contentedly on the hookah.

"So," I asked awkwardly, "what are you smoking?"

"Tobacco," said Jimmy with a clearly facetious grin.

"Wanna smoke?" asked Soup, offering his pipe. "I'm winding down this evening. Think it's almost time to beat the sack." His mangled bedtime metaphor made it sound as if he was off to go and masturbate a pillow.

"Have a seat," said Robert, bluntly.

I took a seat on one of the ends of the couch next to Jimmy. He seemed like the friendliest so far.

"So," began Jimmy, "what brings you to our humble home?"

"Is it rabies?" asked Soup, adding, "'cause I'm not up for getting that again."

"Don't worry, I don't bite."

"He didn't ask if you bit. He asked if you had rabies," Robert snorted.

Jimmy turned his grin on me. "Don't mind him," he said, "Robert's a good guy. He just takes some getting used to, is all."

"No worries," I said.

"So seriously, why you here?" The question came from Soup exhaling a large hit of hookah into the room as he spoke and coughing a little after the words had escaped.

"Dirk's helping me out in a jam I guess, like he said."

"What kind of jam?" asked Jimmy.

"Strawberry," I replied with a grin of my own.

Nothing. Not even a giggle.

"You aren't very funny, are you?" Robert finished off his comment by looking away from me and putting the pipe to his lips.

"Maybe you aren't very..." damn! I had started a sentence I didn't have an ending to. "Laughy?" I tried.

Robert continued to not look at me as he smoked and spoke, "Guess that answers that question."

Wanting to move the subject as far away from myself as possible I asked, "So, uh, what were you guys talking about before we got here?"

"Time," said Jimmy. "Soup was telling us a story, weren't ya, Soup?"

Soup nodded, now beginning to look a little green around the gills. "Might have to save it for another time," he said. "I'm not feeling my best."

"Aw come on," chided Jimmy. "It won't take long to finish."

"Yeah, but I gotta restart on accounta the new guy."

"Boo hoo," said Robert, now looking intently at the back of his hand. "Man, I totally don't know anything like the back of my hand."

"It'll take a second," Jimmy prodded, "come on!"

"All right, all right. Get off my ass, will ya?"

"So time?" I asked.

"Yeah," Soup began, "we were talking about time. I don't remember how we got started or anything, but that's what we ended up talking about and it reminded me of this one time I tried to live without time hanging over my head all the time... man I said time a lot of times just now."

His color had started to return as he spoke, his skin seeming to glow a little with the attention he was getting.

"So, what happened was, is that I was in this video store with this girl I was seeing. We were browsing for about an hour and had finally settled on something and then we go up to the front to pay and there's this line stretching like, literally the whole length of the store. So, we find our way to the back and I'm agitated because I have to wait and I hate waiting, always have... maybe it's a condition or something...

"Anyhow, we are now sandwiched into the middle of the line, and... hey, who's heard this part already?"

"Aye," said Jimmy.

Robert raised his hand, still staring at the other one. I was amazed he was hearing anything at all. His hand must have been fascinating.

"One of you, get me a drink."

"I'll do it," moped Jimmy, getting up. He disappeared around the corner. Soup waited until he was gone to continue.

"So we're standing in line and I'm getting grumpy, twitchy and all that, and it hits me like a fist in the nuts: I'm paying for this. I'd just had like, a forty hour work day..."

Jimmy re-entered the room with a can of pop, "Soup likes to exaggerate."

"I *never* exaggerate."

Jimmy laughed and handed him the can.

"You call this a drink?"

"It's liquid isn't it?"

"It isn't thirst quenching! Couldn't you get me some lemon water or something?"

"Yeah, I'll just go cut you a nice slice of lemon. Drink's a drink."

"I would've settled for just water even."

"So you just worked a 'like, forty hour work day'?" Robert reminded him.

"Like I was saying," Soup continued, giving Jimmy a sidelong glare as he did, "I had just worked all day so that I could do what? Make money. And I was using that money so that I could do what? Buy gas to drive my car, pay for my insurance, hell, *buy* the damn car, and so forth with all the car bull. And then I use that money, to go and pick up my girlfriend, drive to the movie store to do what? Spend an hour of my time, not including the time in the line up, to pay for *two more hours of my time watching the bloody movie!*"

"Yeah," I shrugged. "They say time is money."

Soup gave me a look that made me wish I'd stuck to keeping my mouth shut and listening. "Yeah. We all know that. This is not only about that though, okay? Well, it is, but it's more about my own personal realization of that. I was accepting a truth." He looked around the room as if we were an audience of more than three and said, "Am I okay to continue? Is that... no, no really I'm good? Well all right then!"

He sighed loud enough to kill a librarian before resuming his tale.

"So here I am, in the line, really pissed off now, and we finally get up there and I begrudgingly hand over my movie rental card and my cash and we head out to the car and drive back to my place.

"We pop in the movie, get a couple of drinks, start to relax, it's all looking good. I'm starting to forget about the time bullshit and then I hear it. My girlfriend's leaning up against me and I'm at the arm of the couch and her hand is like, here, on my chest," he moved one of Jimmy's hands to his chest to simulate the affectionate position.

Jimmy jerked his hand back to join the other one at the hookah. "Jesus, man!"

Soup ignored him and continued, "And her watch is on that hand! It's close enough to me that every now and then I hear this *'tick tick tick tick tick tick tick'*, and I'm not about to move her hand, cause, you know… bad move.

"The movie's starting to get interesting at this point and I'm becoming more involved but I keep hearing it creep in, and after a while, it's all I can hear! The movie's gone, we weren't even watching it anymore, it was just that ticking sound. But that's not even the worst of it, no way, man. The worst of it was is that I was wearing my watch too and the more I became aware of hers ticking, the more I started to notice mine ticking! And my ticking's just a little out of sync, like it's playing catch up with hers in the race to drive me fucking crazy and then all I hear is both watches going *tickick-tickick-tickick- tickick- tickick- tickick- tickick- tickick- tickick- tickick- tickick- tickick- tickick- tickick* and it's making me mental!

"So eventually, the evening's over and I drive her home like a gentleman and head back to my place on a mission. On the way, I opened my window and hurled my watch out into the street. I hope it either got run over or is pissing off some stranger who happened to find it. Anyway, I get home, watch-less, and take all of my clocks and begin to stop time for myself. I had enough. I unplugged all my digitals, I took the batteries out of my wall clock and I unplugged my VCR and then plugged it back in so all there was that flashing 12:00. I decided right then and there that I wasn't going to be a slave to time."

"How'd *that* work out for you?" asked Jimmy, taking a tiny toke.

"Fucking sucked," replied Soup, taking a swig. Somewhere along the line, he'd opened the can. "I was late for work 'cause I'd sleep in all the time, I missed the shows I liked to watch, I'd go to the store when it was past closing even though I knew what time the store closed, blah, blah, blah. The worst of it was the missing work part. I had to actually make up my time so in the end I decided that it wasn't worth it."

"Deep," said Robert, gazing at his hand.

"Knee deep," I intoned, foolishly.

More silence greeted my bad joke and then, after a pause that seemed far too long, came this, from Robert:

"Cheesebomb!"

"What's a cheese bomb?" asked Jimmy with a snort.

"Dirk said buddy needed a nickname. I just gave him one."

"I'm not a big fan of Cheesebomb," I said.

"You don't get to pick your nickname," Jimmy said, face still split with a beaming row of teeth.

"He's right you know," agreed Soup. "I'm afraid he's right."

"Why Cheesebomb?" I asked.

"Cause your jokes are cheesy and they always seem to bomb. Ergo, Cheesebomb," explained Robert.

There were a round of 'Ahhhhh's' and then Jimmy said, "Agreed."

"So it's settled," said Soup, "Cheesebomb it is."

"That's a stupid name," I said, digging the hole a little deeper.

"Why?" asked Robert. "Not, gouda-nuff for you?"

They all bloody laughed.

"Oh, so it's funny when he does it..."

"It's the *way* he does it!" laughed Jimmy. "Man, don't worry about it. It's all gouda!" They cracked up again.

"That's the same fucking joke," I mumbled.

Thankfully, Dirk came back in.

"Hey, what's so funny in here?" he asked, hands on his hips and a smile on his face.

"Cheesebomb! Dude's nickname is Cheesebomb!"

Dirk nodded with a thoughtful expression, "Good name!"

"He doesn't think so, do ya Cheesebomb?"

"Dirk?" I pleaded... well, half pleaded. It was said in more of a "What the hell is up with these guys?" kind of way.

"Explain it to me later," Dirk told the associates. "We've got business to attend to." He motioned for me to follow him. "Come on!"

I got up, no doubt red faced, more than a little irritated and happy to be leaving.

Dirk led me into the kitchen and from there, the kitchen table.

"Seriously," I asked, "What's up with those guys?"

"Don't mind them," he said, "they take a bit of getting used to, but they're great once you get to know them."

"I'll bet," I sniffed.

"Lighten up. Hey, listen, I've got our plan sort of figured out and it can start as early as tomorrow. In fact, it *will* start as early as tomorrow. So let's get to tomorrow as fast as we can! What time is it?" Dirk looked around as if he'd never looked at a clock in his own kitchen before.

I looked over, found the microwave and reported, "8:30."

"AM or PM?"

I sighed once again. "PM."

"You know Cheesebomb, you're really going to have to stop that sighing. It's very unbecoming."

"Don't call me that."

"Don't sigh."

"I'm not making any promises."

"Then neither am I."

Sigh

"Cheesebomb."

"Fuck!"

"Chill out! Here, I'll show you your room. It's cleaner than anticipated."

Dirk led me out of a different door than the one we had come in and down a hallway. We stopped in front of a plain wooden door with a poster of Strawberry Shortcake on the outside.

Pointing at the ridiculous childhood paraphernalia, I simply asked, "Dirk?"

"What? It's Strawberry Shortcake! What's wrong with Strawberry Shortcake?"

I gave him a look.

"Beggars can't be choosers. The poster stays. Now open up!"

I did. Thankfully, the poster was not an indication of what the room was like. It was plain, furnished with only a bed and a nightstand. Dirk had already moved my bags and boxes in. The fact that my entire life seemed to fit neatly into one corner of the room was a little depressing.

"Looks pretty good, huh?"

I had to admit, it did.

"So, what time tomorrow morning?"

"I'm not sure yet. Get to bed," said Danger. "I'll see you in the AM."

"That sounds like a plan. I am a little weary."

"Good show! Have a sweet sleep there, Cheesebomb."

And with that, he was gone.

Five

Lesson 1:
A Well Deserved Humbling

"GET UP, YOU FREELOADING, HONKY DOUCHEBAG!" These words, coupled with a splash of water to the face, were a sudden alarm clock.

"What the hell? Where am I?" I sat bolt upright in bed and looked around frantic and bewildered. Dirk was standing over my cot holding a towel in one hand and a recently emptied glass in the other.

"I've been trying to get you up for about fifteen minutes now," he said. "Figured I'd resort to more, shall we say, Dangerous tactics?" One of his eyebrows arched mischievously as he tossed the towel into my face. "Get up!"

Wiping the water out of my eyes I glanced over at the actual alarm clock.

"It's ten o'clock in the morning," I whined. "On a Saturday."

"Danger waits for no man. It's time for your first lesson. Come on, I've got breakfast made. Danger special: sausage wrapped in a bacon *avec l'œuf.*"

"Bacon and eggs?" I asked.

"Sausage wrapped in a bacon and eggs," he said, rolling his eyes and departing my room. "GET UP!"

I literally rolled out of bed and hit the floor, slightly damp and more than a little miffed. At least there were eggs.

In the kitchen, Danger was wearing an apron that said "KISS THE DANGER!" exclamation point and all.

"Did you get that apron custom made?" I asked, sitting down at the table in front of a plate that had been laid out.

"No, I found it in an alley on a sleeping homeless man who didn't even stir as I took it off of him and gave him a swift kick for good measure."

I stared at him blankly.

"Yes, I had it custom made. How do you like your eggs?"

"Scrambled," I said.

"Well that's too bad," he grinned. "These aren't scrambled at all." He brought a frying pan from the stovetop over to my seat and scooped out a couple of eggs over easy onto my plate. "I'll grab you a sausage wrapped in a bacon, hold on." He went back to the stove, grabbed a second pan and dumped two of the aforementioned meat medleys onto my plate next to the eggs.

"Is there a name for these things?" I asked, prodding the bacon/sausage with a fork.

"Yeah, I call them sausage wrapped in a bacon."

"No, I know, but like, a real name. Like toad in the hole, or... pig keeping the secret or something."

He gave me a look, put down the pan and put his hands on his hips. "What secret?"

"What the sausage is made of. I don't know what's in a sausage. Do you?"

"Meat. Now eat it and stop griping."

"But I'm not..."

"Eat! We don't have time for idle chit chat. Idle chit chat is scheduled for this evening."

I shrugged and dug in.

43

When we had finished eating Dirk looked at me quite seriously and said, "You'd better get ready. We have life to learn."

He got up and cleared the table as I left the room to go and fix myself up for whatever we were about to go and do.

A quick shower and a change of clothes later, I headed to the living room and noticed the absence of the Associates.

"Hey Dirk?"

"Mmmmmyes?" he said, appearing in the doorway on the other side of the living room.

I gestured at the couches.

"Oh, they're out for the day. Saturday is fresh air day. They all go to the park, find a nice copse of trees and smoke weed there. Ready to go?"

I shrugged. "Yeah, I guess. Where are we going?"

"If I told you it would ruin the mystique. Just pretend our journey is like the eating of a sausage. You have no idea where it came from, but it sure is exciting to wonder!"

Before I could respond to that he added, "Got any money? Well, how much is left anyway?"

"I don't know. I think I have a hundred or so on my bank card and about 5 bucks in change."

"That'll be enough for now. Bring the change and the card."

"What am I buying?"

"Can't tell you that either. Mystery. Now let me get this Dangerous apron off and we can get the bleeding shit out of here!"

He disappeared back into the kitchen, emerging only moments later by jumping into the room like he was playing hop scotch. "Get your coat! And your money!"

I obeyed and we were on our way.

We walked in silence for a few moments before I asked again, "*Where* are we going?"

"Shhh."

"Seriously, this is childish."

"No, it's intense. You are curious, and keep asking your questions. I'm defiant, stoic, refusing you access to knowledge that will only unfold before you. You want to know and I'm not telling and I seem content to say nothing at all so you, uncomfortable, await the future in awed reverence!"

"Something like that."

We continued on in silence. It became clear that we were heading for a train station. I didn't bother asking to confirm, knowing he wouldn't say anything either way.

Sure enough, we soon sauntered on up to the neighbourhood LRT platform.

"Pay for your ticket my friend. Won't cost you more than a dime and a dollar."

"It's two fifty," I said, making my way to the ticket machine.

"Figure of speech," Dirk replied.

"Since when is 'wrong' a figure of speech?"

"Tuesday."

We bought our tickets and sat down on a bench to await the machine that would take us to our mystery destination.

I took out a cigarette and lit up. "So what are these lessons gonna be like anyway?"

"You shouldn't smoke on the platform. It's a by-law."

"The lessons?" I pushed, "What are they going to be like? Like, are you going to take me to the library and make me read something, or show me an art gallery and give speeches about what all the paintings mean, or are you just going to drop me off somewhere and hope I get the hint?"

He looked over at me calmly. "You are not allowed to smoke here. And also, the lessons are to be learned as we go, with no foreknowledge whatsoever about how they are to unfold. If I did that, it would ruin the whole process. If you want to talk while we head to the lessons, talk about something that's got nothing to do with the lessons. I'd be happy to do that. And you should put that thing out."

"I'm living dangerously."

"No, you're living like you want a $2000 ticket."

"Betcha I don't get caught," I said.

"Betcha I don't really care," he shot back. "It's just that you can't afford a ticket like that right now. And my helping you for the month is not about getting fined. Go wait off of the platform if you're going to smoke." He crossed his arms and sat back.

"Are you coming with me if I go over there?"

No reply.

"Dirk?"

"Shhhh. Stoic."

I mumbled some curse about Jesus and stepped off of the platform. The train showed up almost immediately thereafter. The smoke smouldering on the ground, I leapt onto the platform and got through the doors just in time. Danger was already sitting down, looking out the window.

"You weren't going to wait for me?" I asked, sitting down beside him.

"I knew you were going to make it."

"What if I didn't?"

"Then you would've missed the lesson and would have had to make up for the loss. Not my problem."

I sat back, and turned my attention to the other passengers. There were few people on the train with us. There was an older, balding guy in a suit who looked like he would rather be on an island. There was a mother with a child of around three years of age; she reading a book, the kid punching the window with a tiny useless fist. There was a scraggly guy sleeping on a seat, his body curled into the fœtal position, his shoes on the ground and his back facing the other passengers. Dirk smiled sadly at the sleeping man, fondly almost.

There was also a woman that I kept sneaking looks at. She wore black clothing head to toe, and the only places that contained an absence of black were areas that showed off a whole lot of skin. She had a low cut shirt on, a short skirt, knee high boots (with heels!), black hair and a cute little black hat. I nudged Dirk.

"Hey Dirk," I half whispered.

He gave me an eyebrow.

"Check out that girl." I nodded in the woman's direction.

Immediately I regretted saying a damn thing.

Dirk got up and headed over to her.

"Dirk, hey! No..." I hissed at him as he looked back and shrugged.

He made his way over to the girl and sat down.

She gave him a look that said, "Who the fuck are you?" and waited for him to say something.

"Madam," he began. I put my face in my hands.

"Madam, my Associate over there has been giving you the once over. He finds you attractive and I wish to embarrass him, so, if you would be so kind, could you go over to him and explain exactly why you have no interest in him whatsoever?"

I looked up through my hands in time to see her shrug, get up and swish her way over to my seat. She put her hand under my chin, lifted my face to meet her gaze and said, "First of all, I have a boyfriend. Second, I don't think you're cute, and third, I'm not going to go out with anyone I meet on the fucking train? 'Kay?" She swished her way back to her seat, gave Dirk an "Are you happy?" look, holding her arms out in inquisition, and he nodded, got up and came back to me.

"Not cool man," I muttered, trying not to notice the other passengers, however few there were, smirking away at me.

"Free lesson," Dirk said. "Don't treat every attractive lady you see like an object. Makes you look like a pig. You'll just end up embarrassing yourself. And you aren't ever going to meet a stranger on a train. Now sit tight while we get where we're going."

For the rest of the ride, I sulked, and tried to keep a pout from my face.

WE GOT OFF THE train at one of the bigger malls in town.

"My lesson's at a mall?" I asked with a snort, still fuming from my embarrassment on the train. "What the hell are we going to learn here?"

"Oh, you'll see. And then, we'll hit the food court. And if we have time, one more special stop off. But first, the lesson. Now let's go! I hope they're there." With that, he took off and left me to follow, and with a sigh, I did.

"Should I bother asking who you hope is there?"

No reply.

We arrived at the top of an escalator and Danger looked around for a moment.

He tapped his lip with his index finger and muttered, "Now which mallway was it... ?"

"Mallway?"

"Figure it out."

Another sigh slipped through my lips.

"AHA!" Dirk's index finger shot into the air and he rushed into the closest 'mallway'. I followed him in and walked up to where he stood, facing the window of a games store.

"So this is where the lesson is to be learned, is it?" I asked him.

He nodded. "Look," he said and pointed inside.

The games store was loaded with Dungeons and Dragons books, dice and trading cards displayed in glass showcases at the till, walls filled with pewter modeling kits and hand crafted action figures. In the center of this realm of geekdom sat its kings. A table had been set up in the middle of the store and around it was seated a motley crew of nerds in various forms of outcast attire. They wore glasses, hound's-tooth sweaters, jeans far too tight, slicked hair or hair with terrible cuts, unkempt fingernails, even a bowtie. One guy was wearing rubber boots if you can believe it. I sure as hell couldn't, because the first thing out of my mouth was:

"Is that guy wearing rubber boots? I can't believe it."

"Believe it."

"Why are we here?"

"To watch these guys for a while."

They were playing some sort of strategy game with carefully painted pewter figurines. The playthings were kept in better condition that the players. Dice was rolled and pieces moved here and there. Machine gun noises escaped their pursed lips, globules of spit exiting with the imagined bullets and RAT-A-TAT sound effects. They made karate chop moves, fake kicks and drank soda with jerked sips from the can. Each and every movement made was awkward and looked as if they were practicing movement, working towards mastery. There was even the occasional snort. Textbook geekery.

Danger watched these kids with a huge grin on his face.

"I don't get it," I said.

"Look at those guys! They're awesome!"

I shrugged, turning back to look at the dance of the geeks.

After a moment, Dirk said, "Wouldn't you just love to hang out with those guys?"

"No, not at all," I replied without hesitation.

"Yeah, me neither."

Another pause.

"Then why are we here?"

"Because they love hanging out with each other. These kids are people that get picked on for being different and nerdy, but they all have that in common, so they stick together and enjoy their common interests."

"And... ?"

"And you'd told me at the airport that you felt you didn't belong anywhere. You'd said that you had a problem finding friends because you didn't have anything in common with anyone. And I'm here to tell you that these geeks solve your problem after a fashion."

"But I told you I don't want to hang out with these people," I said. "They're nothing like me."

"That's the point! There's someone out there for everyone. You, me, even these societal outcasts have found solace in each other. I wish I could take every kid that got picked on and felt alone in the world and sit them in front of this window, urge them to go on inside and be friends. These people are the easiest people in the world to make friends with. All you have to do is show interest.

"Right now in the mall, there's a gaggle of girls shopping for clothing and saying 'like' every few words. There's a group of guys scoping the mall for those girls. There's popular kids, unpopular kids, kids dressed head to toe in black, kids with piercings who wear too much plaid, mothers, fathers, business associates on lunch break... there's someone for everyone, and there's someone for you. Probably not at the mall though. You don't seem like a mall guy. We're just here to illustrate my point."

And he did have a point.

"So," I asked, "Who's out there for me?"

"That," he said, "You'll have to figure out for yourself. Our next lesson will take us to a place that might be helpful to you though..."

My mouth open, he anticipated the question and immediately said, "Don't bother asking. You'll see."

And with that, Danger turned back to the window, made the Vulcan live long and prosper symbol with his fingers and pressed his hand against the glass in a solemn solute.

I shrugged and did the same.

Six

Dirk Danger Loves Music

"So what kind of music do you like anyway?"

Dirk posed this question to me in the music store at the mall. We had wandered in after our quiet salute to geekdom. Dirk was fixing to find me some soulful new tunes.

"Music is a necessary thing in our lives today. I can't imagine how I ever got along without it. Music lifts you up when you're down, relaxes you, brings out emotions usually reserved for conflict situations and above all, allows you to relate to someone who feels how you feel," he had explained.

The music store was ruled by a different little subculture of youngsters, far removed from the gadabout hilarity of the D&D folk in the games store. These were the apathetic types who had watched *High Fidelity* and *Empire Records*, liked what they saw and acted accordingly. They were the most practiced crowd of people in the whole of the mall, and quite frankly, the only people I could see myself easily becoming friends with. These angry youths, these suburban socialite children in pauper's clothing, these confused and troubled pop culture elitists — these were my kind of human beings. Pulp's "Common People" should be the only song allowed to be broadcast through the store. These *faux* failures reeked of self pity and only the vaguest idea of what the term 'customer service' even implied. I got a kick out of the whole play. In my experience, for every one truly gifted music store employee who really cares about music, who really has a passion for it and loves to discuss it, there are a dozen other teenagers who were there simply because they figured that they should be. For every one mini-musicologist there were a great wad of snivelling weirdoes who would audibly snort if you brought up to the counter an album they disparaged.

Dirk and I waded our way to the 'ROCK' section and began to rummage.

"I've always liked alt-rock," I told him. "A true child of the nineties."

Dirk gave me an odd look. "You know," he said, "Mariah Carey had more hit music in the nineties than any of those alt-rock grungies. What makes you think that they define the nineties and Mariah Carey doesn't?"

"Mariah Carey is the antithesis of the nineties," I said, growing slightly angry. "She was a corporate entity, a product. The music that should define our culture, our generation, cannot possibly be someone so thickly doused in gloss that she barely resembles anything other than a walking set of tits with a pretty voice. This whole corporate things bleeds down too, and now you get people like that chick that seated us at the airport bar, just a big syrupy smile and a voice to match. It's all so soul-less. Jesus man, that just ain't right."

"I'm happy to have touched a nerve," Dirk beamed. "I'm glad to see you still have passion for something buried deep within your heart."

"I've got plenty of passion," I said. "Just not a lot of faith. Especially not where my own abilities are concerned." I picked up a copy of *OK Computer*. "Now this, *this* is what the nineties are all about. This album is nothing but alienation and fear. Let the good times roll." I set the album back down and picked up another by REO SPEEDWAGON. "I assume this is more your speed?"

"Hah! Funny stuff big guy. You're a regular Arnold Swarzenegger of comedy, you know that? Remember *Twins*? Now *that* was what the nineties were all about."

"It might've been if *Twins* had come out in the nineties."

"Whatever."

I rolled my eyes. "What exactly constitutes music to you then?"

"I'm sure you won't be surprised to learn that I'm not that much different from yourself in terms of preferential musical likings and dislikings. I too was a fan of the grunge and the horror of alt-rock, but I find that it doesn't play well on repeat listens. I find the music of the nineties is like that pair of ripped blue jeans that you thought was so cool in junior high, but now seems like an embarrassing memory you'd rather forget."

"You know, I never really thought about it, but I suppose ripped jeans and plaid, button-up flannel shirts are like the bell bottoms and platforms of our generation."

"You forgot Doc Martens. Yeah, it's all the same. History repeats itself over and over, it just has a bad eye for fashion is all."

"So what then, you were a Nirvana man?"

"Eh, no."

"Smashing Pumpkins?"

Dirk shook his head.

"Don't tell me you're a Pearl Jam kind of guy..."

"Wrong again," he said.

"Really?" I asked. "I always thought that every nineties music fan could be divided into one of three groups. There were the truly depressed Nirvana fans, the sometimes depressed, more whimsical Pumpkins fans and finally, the uh... Pearl Jam fans, which are not so much depressed as depressing."

Dirk wandered over to where the Pearl Jam albums were stored. "Come on now, Vedder's not so bad a guy."

"It just works into my equation that way. If you're a fan of one band, you probably have a little respect for one of the remaining two, and want nothing to do with the third. I was a Nirvana fan, so I had a little respect for the Pumpkins and none at all for Pearl Jam. It's just politics is all."

"So you must like Pixies then?"

"Who?"

"Wow. I'm shocked." Dirk reached past the Pearl Jam and unearthed an album by the Pixies entitled *Doolittle*. "You've never heard of Pixies? Really?"

"Nay." I said, shaking my head slightly.

"Neigh is for horses," he replied. "What about Neil Young?"

I shook my head again. "What did Neil Young ever have to do with alt-rock. I can do without hearing 'Harvest Moon' ever again. That song drives me nuts."

"Neil Young," Dirk said with great seriousness, "is the *godfather* of all grunge music."

"Right. And Mariah Carey is the godmother of the Spice Girls, who are the nurse maids of All Saints, or All Spice or whatever the hell they were called."

"Seriously," he said with a face that looked both shocked and serene with curious consternation at the same time. "Neil Young is the godfather of grunge music. I've got an album for you to buy. Well, two actually. You're getting this Pixies one too. I can't believe you didn't know that. And you call yourself a Nirvana fan."

I had never before made any connection with the hard and angry grunts of alt-rock guitar with the mournful wail of Neil Young's most signature warble. When I thought of Neil Young I though of acoustic guitars, calm and soothing imagery.

"Did you know that Neil Young is Canadian?" Dirk asked me as he flipped idly through the C — section.

"I did not. Did you know William Shatner is Canadian?" I shot back in a lame attempt at one-upmanship.

"Everyone knows that William Shatner is Canadian. The man's a national treasure, for Christ's sake. William Shatner is as much a Canadian symbol as the beaver or the maple tree."

Well fine, then, I thought. "What does Neil Young being Canadian have to do with anything anyway?" I figured that if I couldn't appear to be knowledgeable of famous Canadians, I could at least brush off the idea that knowing this sort of thing could have any useful function.

"It's just neat to see how little it gets noticed that certain groups or individuals are from our little country. We get so incorporated into the American way we sometimes quite literally forget who we are. Or at the very least, we never know at all that we were growing up alongside them all along. Neil Young found his major success in America and so, we learned of him from within America, not Winnipeg, or wherever he's from. Did you know, the Tragically Hip..."

"Are Canadian, yes."

"Uh, I was going to say that they aren't played all that often on American radio. They're like our best kept secret. But yeah, I guess the fact that they're Canadian is kind of important to that sentiment. We get so much of our media from the States that we don't really know, or aren't really able to discern, what info is coming from where. When the Tragically Hip are played right next to some American rock band on Much Music we assume that they must get the same stuff down there that we do up here. Totally not the case. The Americans keep foreign influence out, but they send out whatever they can of themselves. We take things in, send little out and become confused as to what it really means to be Canadian when we realize that after so much has been let in, Canadian culture is something of a chameleon. We're like one great shrug.

"I also brought up Neil Young's heritage because it's interesting to see how we influence the world without, as you can attest, not knowing it's us that's doing it."

"I guess," I said.

Dirk picked up a copy of some Chantal Kreviazuk CD and tsk-tsked. "Now, here's another Canadian. She shouldn't be allowed to reside in the rock section though."

I took the CD from Dirk and waved it at one of the clerks, whose enlarged earlobes could have been rented to the local aquarium for dolphin shows.

"What?" asked the clerk. It was an expected response, and I suppose appropriate as well, seeing as how what I was doing to get his attention was the equivalent of snapping one's fingers at a waitress or whistling at a woman sashaying her way along the sidewalk.

"What's this doing in the rock section?" I asked.

"I can't even see what it is," he grumbled.

I brought it over to him. "Look, see? How can this be."

He shrugged. "Write a letter," he suggested.

"To whom?"

"How the hell should I know?"

Apparently, this clerk was not one of the passionate few.

Returning to Dirk, who was still burrowing through the C-section, I plunked the CD randomly into the mix. "Maybe no one will find it?" I suggested hopefully.

"You ready to get out of here?" Dirk asked.

"You know it, honkey."

I paid for my CDs — the Pixies album and a copy of Neil Young's *Rust Never Sleeps* — which I wasn't too pleased about, and we headed off back to the train station.

The day had turned slightly cold, a thin wind sneaking its way into my cotton clothing with graceful ease. Warm thoughts of coffee percolated in my head. I settled on a cigarette for the time being.

"Why do you smoke?" Dirk asked, looking back at me after I had stopped walking to shield my enfeebled lighter from the breeze.

"Why do you care?" I asked through clenched teeth, lips half full of tobacco filter.

"Just curious. Indulge me."

I had succeeded in lighting the tip of my tube of temporarily solidified smoke and celebrated with a lung warming inhale. "Everyone's got a vice. Mine's tobacco."

"And coffee, and... pornography..." he added with a shudder. "But *why* do you smoke cigarettes. Having a need for a vice is hardly a reason."

"Well, it's... stupid, actually."

"So what?"

"You'll think I'm ridiculous."

"I already do."

"Well, I told you I want to be a writer," I began. "In my head, a writer is a tortured individual. A writer is someone who drinks too much whiskey, smokes too many cigarettes, chases all the wrong women for all the wrong reasons and also, wears a fedora and a wrinkled jacket. I'm filling a portion of my quota." I adjusted my tie with my free hand for emphasis.

"Seriously?" he asked as we boarded the train platform and I was forced to extinguish my cigarette.

"Yeah. Stupid, huh."

He nodded vigorously. "Very much so."

"Thanks for the boost," I said.

"You know," Dirk mused, "you think you might be fulfilling some destitute self-fulfilling prophecy with your life sucking situation."

"How do you mean?"

"I mean I think that part of the reason you aren't trying to succeed as a human being is because you've built up this aura around who you want to be, this notion that you need to be a person who suffers. You need to be a person that has it bad so that you'll have something to write about. You feel like you need to build character by failing on purpose because you assume that's what you're supposed to do to be a successful writer. Any credence? Or am I just flailing my verbal limbs madly?"

I shrugged. "Doubt it."

"I don't know about that. You know, I kind of assumed you liked bleak nineties rock. I had a hunch."

"Hardly a tough thing to divine," I said.

"Don't you think that your musical tastes might have something to do with your inability to function as a human being?"

"That is singularly one of the most stupefyingly ridiculous questions I've ever been asked." I responded. "I suppose then that the game Doom really is responsible for most of today's youth violence."

"It's not like that," Dirk said, thrusting his arms behind his back and pacing to and fro along a short section of train platform. "You see these rockers, these Kings of Sonic Distortion, and you like what you see. You see these tortured poets, these people that seem as if they can barely dress themselves and you feel their music deeply. It touches you, reaches out to you. You yearn to be profound and powerful just like they are and to do so, you feel like you should be emulating them, living the life you expect that they had led — breeding pain to build art."

I said nothing.

"Of course, most famous writers worth their salt lived no better. At least Hemmingway had a nice place in Cuba."

The train pulled up and we rode the rails home in relative silence.

THE ASSOCIATES WERE STILL not home. It was only about three in the afternoon when we arrived back at Le Manse du Danger. Dirk requested I throw on a CD while he made a pot of coffee. "Stereo's in the living room," he said.

I took the CDs out of their cello wrap and gave them the once over. The cover of the Pixies album was brown and sl ightly uninviting. There was a little drawing of a monkey and a few encircled numbers all floating in dark brown relief. The track listing contained songs with titles like "La La Love You" and "Crackity Jones". I was more curious about this album than I was about the Neil Young one, having heard Young's songs on the radio over and over again. I put on the Pixies album as Dirk arrived with a steaming mug of extra strong black bean soup.

"You've really never heard of this band?" he asked, setting my coffee down on the table.

"Nope," I said as the CD loaded, the first bars of the opening track "Debaser" filtering into the room. We listened for a while to the crashing cacophony and sweet little melodies, the bizarre squealing of the lead singer and the buried humour bubbling to the surface. I was quite struck by the album. So struck in fact, that I found myself eagerly awaiting the next track, wondering what surprises it had in store. "La La Love You" was one of my favourites. It undercut someone professing deep love to a background chant of "First Base, Second Base, Third Base, Home Run!", sneaking in the bleak way in which the words are often used. The whole of the album was a jubilant mess, a quiet masterpiece.

"This is fantastic!" I said. "I can't believe I've never heard them before."

"I picked them up because you mentioned you liked Nirvana. Neil Young too. Kurt Cobain was a huge fan of the Pixies. He borrowed their dynamic, the way the songs alternate between quiet intimacy and blistering shrieks of guitar and voice. But I picked them up for another reason as well."

"And that is?"

"Well, I wanted to show you that the music you say defines your generation doesn't have to be that bleak stuff you clung to so happily. This is where that music came from and as you can see, it is a funny, giddy place to be. Cobain took the bits and the pieces and, with his regrettably troubled mind, made a different kind of music, a kind of music that took off and made kids like you pout your teenaged years away. It doesn't have to be bleak is all."

"Why the Neil Young?"

"Listen to the last track on that album you bought. It's the flipside of a famous Neil Young track. The famous version is the first track on the album. Cobain quoted Neil Young in his suicide note, you know."

"I didn't know," I said. "I never got too into the Cobain death thing. I thought it was pretty disrespectful. What was the quote?"

"It's better to burn out than to fade away."

"Ah, that one."

"Yeah, the song it's from is beautiful, and it's counterpoint, the last song on that album there, is a heavy, crunching master work. It proves that Neil Young knows a thing or two about the term 'ahead of his time'."

"I thought you weren't trying to depress me," I said.

Dirk smiled. "I don't interpret the lyrics the way some do. I see it as a call to know when to quit. Young also says in the one version, 'It's better to burn out cause rust never sleeps'. I see that as a warning not to overdo what ever it is that you do. *Seinfeld* is a good example. The show ended before it got stale. They could have kept slogging on, but Jerry recognized that if they kept doing that and got stale, people would remember the decline and forget the good times. Young, in a more eloquent way, was saying 'quit while you're ahead'. I think Cobain knew that as well, he was just extremely depressed and people took the words more in the context of his death than in their meaning."

Doolittle was winding down.

"Try not to take things so seriously," he said.

"I suppose that's good advice."

We listened as the album played out and then sat in silence for a while. Dirk was right about me. I was a self-fulfilling prophecy of doom. At least I knew it now.

Seven

Lesson 2:
At Dave's Heavy Artillery and Bakery

"**Y**OU DID WHAT?"

"I signed you up."

Day three with Dirk. The day had been relatively uneventful. I was home alone for the majority of the morning and most of the afternoon, during which time I had watched television and indulged my habits. Dirk had gone out somewhere and I could only wait until he returned to find out what was on the agenda for the day. Danger strolled through the door at around five and dragged me right out of the house. In no time at all, we ended up where we currently were, a small restaurant called *Dave's Heavy Artillery and Bakery*.

The building was divided in two. One half was the bakery portion where one could go for a nice loaf of sourdough or a dozen croissants. We were in the second half, the restaurant portion. It was as bizarre a place as I've ever been. The walls were adorned with old American propaganda posters. The phrase 'BUY WAR BONDS' was littered all over the walls accompanied by varying images of soldiers holding rifles or fighter jets flying *en masse* to some dire event. There was one poster in particular that advertised a laundry detergent that helped fight the war on communism. In and among the posters were gun replicas hung up on the walls along with ammo belts strung underneath the odd rifle giving the whole set up a 'skull and crossbones' feel. The serving staff all wore army fatigues and black berets, their names swaying from their necks on dog tags instead of nametags. At the back of the restaurant stood a stage that was currently concealed by a heavy silver curtain decorated with rivets painted on along the middle, dividing it in two. Above the curtain hung a banner on the ceiling that advertised "The Iron Curtain Stage" in bold letters. And then there was the menu. I liked it so much I reprinted it here for your enjoyment:

Dave's Heavy Artillery & Bakery

Because War is as Common as Sliced Bread

Salads

Tossed Greenpeace

We take a traditional green salad and add a violent explosion of fruit flavour! We tossed in some field berries to freak the establishment a little.

4.99

Et Tu Bruté?

Romaine lettuce, oversized croutons, bacon bits and parmesan cheese with our own Red Cæsar Dressing for that added assassination feel.

5.99

Achilles' Heel

It's our only weakness! A medley of pitted olives, rich chunks of Feta cheese, green peppers, cucumbers and cherry tomatoes, served with a tangy Greek dressing.

6.99

Appetizers

Nobel Peace Fries with a Gravy U-Boat

Homemade French fries with our own special seasoning served with a thick gravy on the side.

Individual: 4.99 / To Share: 7.99

Raspoutine

A Dave's favourite! Our homemade fries smothered in cheese and gravy, served with a side of Cossack Vinaigrette for dipping.

Individual – 6.99 / To Share – 9.99

Sub Machine Buns

We take a French loaf, slice it up and coat it in a spicy garlic butter, then bake it in a blend of Asiago and cheddar cheese. We make them bite sized for rapid fire enjoyment!

5.99

Entrees

(all entrees come with your choice of a
side salad or Nobel Peace Fries)

Missile Lunch

Our Daily Lunch Special. A juicy steak sandwich
on our French loaf. Served with your choice of side.
You can get the steak how you prefer, though we do
recommend bloody.

9.99 (available only between
noon and 2PM)

Donair Strike

Tender, spiced donair meat and vegetables drizzled
with tzatziki sauce and wrapped in a thick pita. We
recommend the Achilles' Heel Salad as a side.

10.99

Fidel Casserole

Ground pork, black beans, rice and veggies cooked to
perfection and topped with melted cheddar cheese.

12.99

Bay of Pigs in a Blanket

Thick spiced sausage wrapped in a flaky homemade
pastry and served with a side of black beans on a bed
of rice.

12.99

Beverages

Coffee	1.50
Tea	1.50
Soda	1.99

Beer: Domestic   *4.50*
            Imported   *4.99*

Ask your server about our selection of wines from around the world or try one of our signature martinis made with our Orwellian Victory Gin.

Deserts

Lenin Meringue Pie

Our revolutionary signature dessert with our patented meringue recipe! Each piece is crafted to perfection and drizzled with a bright Red strawberry sauce.

4.99

The Immaculate Confection

A sinful delight! Mounds upon mounds of chocolate and raspberry sauce topped with mango puree and whipped cream.

4.99

Otto von Bismarck's Doughnuts

Four exquisite miniature doughnuts with a thick cream cheese filling and chocolate glaze.

4.99

Chocolate Mussolini

A thick and creamy chocolate mousse made with a helping of wine from the Piedmont region in Italy.

5.49

Condoleezza Rice Pudding

Old fashioned rice pudding with a modern name. Served with a chocolate coated wafer and a dollop of whipped cram. Chilled to perfection.

3.99

AS DIRK HAD EXPLAINED to me, the owner of *Dave's Heavy Artillery and Bakery* was an anti-activist activist, a man who fronted a group of individuals who held the belief that aligning oneself with a group centred on any given ideology was a bad idea.

"Isn't that a contradiction?" I'd asked.

"That's sort of the point," replied Dirk. "It's supposed to comically raise awareness of their concern."

"You'd think it would work against them."

"It probably does."

Dirk had brought me here because, as an easel by the entrance could attest, tonight was 'Bad Poetry Night'. This was what Dirk had signed me up for.

"Why on earth would you sign me up for that? I don't even have a poem with me! What am I supposed to read?"

Dirk reached into his pocket and pulled out a pen. He snatched a napkin up from where they sat in the center of the table and slid it and the pen over to me. "Write one," he said.

I stared at the pen. "I can't just write a poem."

"Why not? It's supposed to be bad. That's the point. That's why I brought you here. This is lesson two."

"Embarrassing the hell out of me is lesson two? Thanks a bunch."

"It's not supposed to be embarrassing! It's supposed to help you get over your fear of expressing yourself publicly."

"Who said I have a fear of expressing myself publicly?" I asked.

"You did. Not in so many words, but it's pretty obvious. You wouldn't let me read your writing, you have trouble relating to others, hence your lack of friends, the no job situation, you..."

"All right, I get it!"

"But seriously, you are going up there. I was here bright and early in the morning to reserve you a spot. You wouldn't believe how popular this event is. There are twenty spots and you're squeaking in at number nineteen. At least you don't have to go last."

"People actually scramble over one another to make fools of themselves?" I asked, looking about for a fatigued waiter or waitress. I was starving and now, in the mood for a drink or two. Dirk had said earlier that dinner was on him, so drinks would have to keep coming... especially if he actually expected me to go up onstage.

Eventually, our server did come. I opted to try one of their Orwellian Victory Gin Martinis. Dirk ordered water. While we waited for our food, Dirk kept prodding me to get writing.

"You don't want to miss the show," he said. "It would be a shame to be trying to write out a poem while the recitation is in progress. It really is something, you should see the characters that get up there..."

Dirk kept talking and aside from the occasional, "Uh-huh" on my part, I didn't really have a place in the conversation. I kept staring at my napkin, pen in hand, gin setling over my brain, and nothing to say.

"Do you need a hand?" Dirk asked.

"Hmmm? Oh, oh, no... I'll get through it... you know I really don't want to go up there. Do I have to do this? I mean... I'm not even prepared... and..."

"Yes, you have to do this. We have an agreement, and I expect you to live up to your end of the bargain."

My mind was racing. I kept running ideas through my brain, but the trouble was, I wasn't trying to write a bad poem. I wasn't a very good poet, but when I tried to write something, I always tried to write something *good*. Writing something bad on purpose is a lot harder than it sounds. I began to write, became unhappy with the ideas that were forming, and I kept thinking, *this isn't bad enough*. I had to wait. I figured it might help if I saw some of the other terrible poets first; saw what passed through their lips to get a better handle on this 'bad poetry' thing.

"Oooo! They're starting!" Dirk squirmed excitedly in his seat.

The Iron Curtain began to open. Erect behind it was a microphone on a long stand, and behind that was a disgusting looking man in a plaid, tweed jacket. His hair was greased back and flat to his scalp and he wore Buddy Holly glasses over his face, lenses on the glasses so thick that his eyes looked like an insect's, darting to and fro to examine the crowd, gauge the turnout. He leaned forward to the microphone with all the grace of a three legged gazelle and spoke:

"Gooooood evening ladies and gentleman! My name is Ceylon Waylon and I'll be your host for the evening! Tonight we have for your dining enjoyment, 20 of the worst poets this city has to offer. There's no telling just how bad things will get, so in case you've forgotten, the bar is to my right."

He paused here for the light laughter that sounded almost as if hyenas stalking the restaurant had chosen to whisper their distinctive cries.

"Well then, without further ado, I bring you your first poet of the evening! May I present, Damien Dagger!"

The crowd applauded and here and there you could hear the excited giggle of those who had been here before, knew what to expect and couldn't wait to get on with the show. I momentarily forgot I had to produce a poem of my own as the first poet took the stage. Ceylon Waylon stalked off and there appeared in his place a man who seemed impossibly tall. His height was exaggerated by knee high leather boots adorned with garish buckles and chains that dangled and shook as he hunted the microphone at the head of the stage. He wore tattered black jeans that were tucked deep into his boots. A cape covered his torso and his thin long black hair hung like curtains on the windows of a haunted house obscuring much of his face, which was painted white with dark circles under his eyes. He glared and bared his teeth as he reached the microphone and flung open his cape, arms extended high in the air. In one of his hands he held a dagger that glinted in the lights of the stage as he held it aloft. Turns out he wasn't wearing a shirt under his cape at all; his lanky, bare chest powdered the same wan colour as his face. He lowered his arms and draped his hair over the microphone. In a deep Jim Morrison baritone he began:

The platypus curled on my hotel pillow
Has eaten the heart shaped chocolate mint
That was left there by youuuuuu... .

THE RAIN!
It beats on my blackened heart,
THE RAIN!

I pour a glass of wine
To toast the demons of my soul
The demons that live in... my eyes
And I raise my cup to the platypus,
Curled like a fist in my memories of youuuuuu...

There is no love here,
Not in this hotel...
Not since you took my wallet,
My heart carefully folded inside,
like a taped up dollar bill,
Not since you cut out my kidney
And left me to rot in a tub full of ice
Like a common salmon,

Sixteen pounds of Coho,
The catch... of a lifetime...

A single tear unfolds from my sight
And wends its way across my scarred visage!
Oh, Tempest, give me strength!
I need the strength to die!
Die for the memory of youuuuuu... .

A knife from the drawer...
Not with my right hand, no,
Not the hand that touched you last,
But with the left hand! And thrust! A dagger to my still
*   born heart...*

The platypus smirks, and its smile,
Its smile is youuuuuuuur'ssssss... .

As his final syllable faded off into the dark of his own personal night he raised the dagger high above his head in both hands and plunged it between his arm and his chest in an overdone pantomime of sorrow and began to stagger about the stage before collapsing in a heap near the edge of the curtain. The man received a standing ovation, full of applause and shouts of "THAT WAS TERRIBLE!" and "GET OFF THE STAGE!" It was a very bizarre juxtaposition, the accolade of clapping met with the jeers from those who clapped the hardest. The enjoyment of something truly awful.

The man in black, Damien, was not getting up. Ceylon Waylon came back out, clapping, and stepped to the microphone. "Wasn't that terrible?" he chided the audience who alternately booed and whistled at the crumpled form onstage. "Why don't you get up and take a bow! Damien Dagger ladies and gentlemen!" Waylon turned to look at the man on the floor, still clapping though the speed of his applause was dwindling. "Uh, Damien?" No answer. Waylon walked over to Damien and whispered something to him. It seemed that Damien was responding but still not moving. A visibly frustrated Waylon sighed, shrugged and began to drag Damien Dagger offstage by one of his boots. Once the man had disappeared completely behind the curtain, Waylon reappeared, panting slightly, and resumed his position at the front of the stage.

"Not bad eh?" Dirk asked.

"It was bloody horrendous!" I replied.

"But everyone loved it, didn't they? You've got 17 more people before it's your turn. Better get writing!"

I glanced back at my napkin and did nothing. I realized I had been unconsciously tapping my pen against my forehead. I stopped my tapping just as a man appeared onstage. I hadn't even heard Waylon announce the next poet. The man was a hulking man with deep black skin and quite possibly the sharpest looking goatee I'd ever seen. He was dressed like a beatnik and his poem was filled with nonsense words to fill in the rhythm of the piece, words like "SKIBA-DEE-DOOO-DOW!" and "BE-BOPPEDEY-KERPOW!" and the like. I had more or less zoned out. I wanted to stay focused on the entertainment but if I didn't get this poem done, I'd be more embarrassed when it came to presentation time.

A few more poets came and went and still I had nothing. I was working on my second Orwellian Victory Gin when the next performer took the stage. Her name was Mary Contrary and she was dressed in a style reminiscent of Alice in Wonderland's blue and white dress. Her hair was in pigtails and she had freckles painted on her cheeks, three on each side and symmetrical. She skipped on stage and as she met the microphone she opened her eyes up wide and I was struck by the colour of them. She possessed the most piercing eyes, a vibrant green, and immediately my poem came to me. I scrawled out the first few lines and was drawn out of concentration again by those eyes of the woman on stage, and her voice as it filled up the room...

The muse of destiny
Visited me today.
She wore a frock and
Smelled like Bengay.

Her wand was homemade
And looked quite ineffectual
And she said she'd just told
Her parents she was a raging homosexual.

"How'd they take it?" I asked
And she burped out some wine
I took that to mean
That they thought it just fine.

"Enough about me!
I'm here about you,
To tell you the future
And play the kazoo..."

And she played it indeed
And she did it quite well
Until she stepped on her foot
And stumbled and fell.

"Sorry, I'm durnk,"
She said incorrectly,
"My head needs a bucket
And it needs it directly."

I fished out a thimble
From deep in a drawer
And she threw up a little
And rolled on the floor.

"So I came here to tell you,
Not to eat so much fat...
It's not good for your health
Or something like that."

"That's all you have to say?"
I asked incredulously.
"I expected so much more
From the wise muse of destiny!"

"Well la-di-dah,
Aren't we so smart!
You probably piss on sticks
And call it high art!"

I couldn't believe that
This imp was so dumb,
So I crushed the muse
With the tip of my thumb.

Her voice was a sing song trill like a starling and to hear her say words like 'piss' and discuss vomit and crushing deaths was obscene! It was as if a toddler from the wrong side of the tracks was up there riffing on violence. But those eyes held me grounded as she sung out her poem and as soon as she stepped off from the stage I began to scrawl madly onto my napkin, getting out my ideas before they had any more time to evaporate. Thank god for those eyes! I could almost feel Dirk's smile as he watched me work.

I finished my poem and looked up at Danger. He still held a grin. "Finished?" he asked.

"Yeah, thanks." I said sarcastically. "Way to turn up the heat."

"It worked didn't it? You're just in time. There's one more to go on before you."

My eyes returned to the stage just in time to see Waylon stepping back and the next poet stepping out. The man wore a woman's stocking over his face like a convenience store bandit. On top of his head was a bowler hat. He was sharply dressed in a suit and despite the stocking obscuring his mouth, his voice carried quite effectively as he recited his brief poem:

> *I laid my eggs in her nest,*
> *And she wouldn't let me incubate them!*
> *"Shit on my chest?" she asked, "Go fuck yourself!"*
> *I said sit, but whatever.*
> *C'est la vie, I thought, and took a sip from my something-*
> *chino.*

Waylon reappeared and my time was up.

"Ladies and Gentlemen! Give it up for Mr. Magritte!" The audience reacted as they had been, clapping and booing as if nodding and shaking their heads at the same time. Waylon continued: "Next up is a new poet to our stage brought to us courtesy of our friend Dirk Danger!" Everyone clapped without booing and Dirk rose and took a bow.

I leaned over to him once he had been seated. "These people know you?"

"No, not most of them. I used to come here quite often in another life. The staff that have been here for a while know me."

My attention returned to Waylon just in time to hear him say, "Ladies and Gentlemen, give it up for Cheeeeesebommmmmmb!"

My newly acquired nickname earned some titters here and there as I snatched up my napkin and shot Dirk a glare. "Bastard," I muttered at him. He shrugged as I stalked off and climbed onto the stage from the front instead of going around through the curtains. I stepped to the microphone and stared down at my napkin. Here goes...

Her eyes are like sapphires,
Stone-ish and sparkly.
Well, maybe they're more like the ocean,
Yeah, vast and with some sharks,
And little green bits that might be kelp or something...
No, no, no!
Like... uh...
Her eyes are like daffodils, except blue and
They don't smell as nice...
Closer, but not close enough...
Maybe they're like,
Big fat blueberries! With a black center...
I guess a worm got in there...
That won't do...
Oh! I got it!
Her eyes are like those earrings my ex used to wear,
They twinkle and sometimes her hair gets caught in
*   them...*
Perhaps I should re-think that a bit...
Maybe they're like teeth that bite into my brain
And won't let go! Huge jagged things that
Get stuck in my head when she shakes my face from
*   side to side*
To get all the juice out...

Or what if they're like sushi!
Delicately crafted, full of raw meat and nice to look at!
Try again...
Of course! They're like two Cyclops' stuck up on her face!
They are the stuff of legends and sometimes they
Throw spears at you...
Or perhaps, her eyes are like two big bottles of beer!
I could drink from them all day,
And they're the first thing I want to see when I get up
  on a Sunday!
Yeah, definitely beer.

I WAS NUMB DURING the whole reading, but I remembered to pace myself and give a pause between the different ideas in the poem. It was pretty bad.

I looked up from my napkin to see the crown give me that same contradiction of a reaction they had given every other poet thus far. It may have been the same damn thing, but it was something to be up on that stage and get the reaction that you wanted, the reaction you expected. I gave a slight bow and moved away from the stage, hopping down off the front and walking past the audience, still clapping, still booing and me, I was smiling away as I approached Dirk and sat back down.

"Good show!" Dirk said. "I knew you'd pull through."

"You're an asshole," I said with a grin and he leaned in for a high five which I returned with an apathetic tap. Danger laughed triumphantly and sat back as the last poet took the stage. Their poem was as follows, introduced as 'The next big thing in romantic poetry':

Roses are red,
I fucked your sister.

Dirk seemed especially fond of that one. He booed and clapped louder than I'd heard him do all night. Maybe he was still flowing with energy because his plan had seemingly worked. He'd got me onstage and he'd given me an appreciative audience.

Damn him if it didn't feel good, too.

Eight

A Painful Labour

"I WANT YOU TO WRITE something."

"Now? Why?"

It was the morning of my fourth day at Dirk's. We were enjoying our morning meal and reminiscing about our night at Dave's Heavy Artillery & Bakery when he hit me with this task.

"We went to the show to help you get over your rejection issue. Did we succeed?"

I looked sullenly into my eggs. "Yeah, in a way."

"Only in a way?"

"Yeah, I mean… it takes more than one night to cure a phobia. It went well and all…"

"You mean it went badly. Which is to say splendidly."

"Uh… yeah…"

"How are the eggs? You look like you're going to be sick on them."

I took a big forkful and shovelled it into my face, placed the utensil down and gave Dirk an "Are You Happy Now?" smile complete with egg laden teeth.

"I don't see why you're so afraid."

"I'm just not in the mood to write."

"What will it take to light that incense in your soul, to get that creative lava lamp a-bubblin'? Do you want to talk about it?"

"About what?"

"About your Ideas!"

"What ideas...?"

Dirk sighed. "I wish you wouldn't be so damn difficult. I know you have Ideas. You don't just call yourself a wannabe writer and not have a few nuggets ready for polishing. So... tell me!"

I had been thinking a lot about sex recently. That was where all my ideas were ending up. I was frustrated. I hadn't had sex in some time, and I had this one idea in particular...

"You're thinking! HUZZAH! What are you dredging up?" Dirk punctuated his outburst with a noisy swig of coffee.

"I..."

"Yes?"

"I've been thinking about sex."

"I thought we'd discussed this. You and I must maintain separate accommodations."

"Not with you! Just... sex in particular."

"With someone specific?"

"No, I'm not fantasizing. It's what I've been thinking about writing about."

Dirk polished off a piece of bacon. "Yeah, I realize that. But are you thinking about you having sex with someone? About someone else having sex?"

"Actually, in my idea, nobody has any sex." I finished off what remained of my eggs while I allowed Dirk to respond.

"Hmmm. So it's about sex, but there's no sex?"

I shrugged. "Haven't written it yet."

"You talk of 'IT'. Do you have a solid Idea or many Ideas?"

"One in particular, but a few that I've been kicking around." I finished off my bacon. Breakfast was over. On to the few sips of coffee I had left, a shallow murky pool in the bottom of my mug.

"What's the one in particular?"

"It's about a pregnant lady."

"Ohhh! Fetish story."

"Not really."

"Well then?"

"It's hard to explain."

"Then let's write it out!"

Dirk finished off his breakfast quickly, too quickly, eager to race up from the table and find me some paper. He shot up, nearly sending his chair toppling to the floor and spun towards the sink, depositing his breakfast refuse and dashing out of the room.

I had a conversation with my remaining coffee.

COFFEE: I'm not good for you. You know that, right?

ME: Why not?

COFFEE: Well, for starters, I thin your blood. Can't be good for you.

ME: Maybe I like my blood thin.

COFFEE: I stain your teeth.

ME: Hardly a health concern. That's just cosmetic.

COFFEE: What about the sugar?

ME: What about it? I like sweet coffee.

COFFEE: It'll rot your teeth. Your teeth will be jet black and then fall out of your head. You want that?

ME: I guess I could use sweetener.

COFFEE: That causes Alzheimer's I heard.

I stared into its thick surface, a bleak and distorted reflection of myself looking back at me.

ME: How did you hear anything at all?

COFFEE: I hear things! What?

ME: Probably just an urban legend anyhow. It's just as well though. I don't like sweetener.

COFFEE: All right, have it your way. Rotting stained teeth are all the rage now I hear.

ME: You're just trying to save your own life. I'm going to digest you and you don't like it.

COFFEE: Now, now! Let's be reasonable! That's not the case at all...

ME: If you could sweat, you'd be drenched.

COFFEE: But I...

ME: Bottoms up, old chum... bottoms up.

GULP

Just as I'd finished, Dirk re-entered the room brandishing a pad of paper and waving a pen out in front of himself like an épée.

"Gonna stab me?" I asked, getting up and putting my breakfast dishes in the sink.

"Nay, pilgrim."

He put the paper and pen on the kitchen table and waved his arm over them as if he'd just magically enabled them to help me write.

"You really think I can just come up with something right here on the spot?"

Dirk chuckled. "No, of course not. You're going to need time to organize your thoughts. That's why you're going to do the following: put on a new pot of coffee, do the breakfast dishes while the coffee's brewing and then take these out to the front stoop and have a few cigarettes while the words come to you."

"Why do I have to do the dishes?"

"Because you're living here for free while I help you. You'll be doing them a lot more often from now on. I wanted you to get settled for a few days before I sprung that on you."

"That's fair I suppose," I grumbled.

"Get started! Find me when you're done. I'll probably be in my room."

"Where are the associates?" I hadn't thought of them until just now. I didn't want them spying on me if I was going to try to write.

"Oh, they're all at work. It's Monday. Now get at it Cheesebomb!"

Dirk leapt out of the room chased by the words, "DON'T CALL ME THAT!" as they rumbled out of my lungs.

I set about my tasks.

Filter — Grounds — Water — Button   ON: Cue percolating noise.

Plug IN — Water ON — Squeeze soap bottle: Cue suds' growth

The time to think did help. Without it, I don't think I'd have put anything on that pad of his. After the first few frustrating plates were clean and drying on the rack I stopped thinking about the dishes altogether and started thinking about my story. It was about a woman. I'd told Dirk she was pregnant and she had been when I'd seen her, but for the purposes of the story, I'd make her a new mother. I'd seen her in a restaurant. I was waiting for something to start, but I couldn't remember what... and I hated the way the restaurant looked... and AND and AND and...

I'd finished the dishes without realizing it. And damned if I didn't have an idea that I could stick on the page. I poured the coffee, added my fixins, rounded up my cigarettes and took the writing utensils to the porch. This is what I came up with:

Nine

The Feel of the River

PEDRO AND I SAT in LOCAL FAST FOOD RESTAURANT eating our Combo #5s while we waited for SPORTING EVENT/MOVIE to begin. It was a good day. Pedro continues from where he left off:

"Yeah, so she just isn't getting me, you know?"

"Yeah..."

I was drifting. Not that I didn't like what Pedro was talking about, or that I wasn't interested; it was just a day for wandering, a day for daydreaming. I was on top of it, floating in and out of consciousness as any little thing distracted me. The tray our food was on displayed pictures of more food. This was appropriate. I applauded how appropriate it was. Good show. The pictures on the walls were not of food. This was also pleasing. Too much food can be a bad thing. Here on the walls were paintings, sort of like those magic eye pictures that you have to look at just right. Like Monet. Sure... whatever.

Pedro had picked up somewhere else by the time I snapped back to him.

"So this guy actually took the cup right out of my hand and took a swig. Man, you should have seen my face..."

Pedro was a good guy, but there were times to talk, and times to drift. This day was a river and I was debris. I had flaked off of some tree upstream and was sailing my way to the ocean on this fine day. Nothing could stop me. Nothing could dam up my way. No bird could fetch me out and use me in its primitive architecture. I was the best kind of debris, free spirited, free thinking, a mouthful of burger and a cup full of sweetener. It was Tuesday.

"And by the time we got kicked out, the guy was long gone so there wasn't a whole lot I can do. You should have seen the girl man, though, like... *fuck!*"

Pedro had done something of note. I could tell. He hadn't eaten much. I nodded, "Yeah, man, I wish I'd seen her..." trailing off, staring past Pedro, my concentration focused on the woman behind him.

She couldn't have been the same 'she' from Pedro's story. For starters, Pedro wouldn't have found her attractive. I knew his type: loose. This one wasn't, hopefully, as she was carrying a child. An infant. Maybe, 6, 7 months old. When I first noticed her I hadn't noticed the child she was cradling in her arms. I was watching the way her jeans cradled her ass. I saw the kid. I was a bit surprised, I mean, she was too slim, too petite to have only recently ejected a child from her body, but...

There she was. It was fact. She held the child between her breasts, overfull and ripe with milk, hiding shyly under a thick blue sweater that she somehow managed to turn into a paper thin negligee using only what she carried beneath it. She bobbed the child, and I tried not to notice her form...

"The guy fucking, goes out there, kicks the bouncer in the teeth..."

"Uh-huh..."

I chew, swallow. The swallow takes too long, forces its way down a throat suddenly too parched to let anything slide. The woman sits, hair resting over the plastic backing of LOCAL FAST FOOD RESTAURANT's child proof seating. My eyes invade her space as the burger finally hits the pit of my stomach with a resonating sting. The grease burrows through to my intestines, gestating, turning from larva into pupa and finally full blown butterfly caressing the lining of my stomach with frantic spasms, hideous tantrums for freedom.

She is motherly, fertile. I cannot bring myself to admit that I am drawn to this woman. She is a mother. A mother has another; one to sow the seeds, to bring home the bacon...

"This is way too salty for me right now. I don't know if I have any antacids..."

Pedro was fond of remedies.

I was fond of afflictions.

She was different now, there beside the play area, the jungle gym...

All of it met with the river, drifting.

The jungle gym was now a full blown jungle, the children within, sock-less vine swingers, climbing under the roots, across the branches, through the tunnels, shouting cries of battle. They wore the skins of animals, wolves, tigers, bears, hyenas. They fought, swatting at one another with paw covered, claw laden hands, screeches and tears becoming more noble somehow, more earthy. The colourful cartoon characters that lined the walls within the jungle had converted themselves into drab and primitive cave scrawling, reminders of ancient times and of humanity's need for expression. Beyond the jungle, the dense vegetation gave way, moving into a clearing where sat this woman, this deity of Amazonian proportions, more than a match for any man. She stood, naked from the waist up, exposed flesh an example of perfection, of nature's truly brilliant talent for creation. Smooth faced and emotionless she surveyed the lands before her, uncaring of her solitude, unafraid of what hardships lay ahead. She was a black widow, only wanting child and not companionship, killing for a little peace and quiet now and again, while her child slept safe and sound between those perfect breasts. I was the unnoticed observer, the inanimate voyeur, the debris on the river that held it all together, that flowed on between the forest and the clearing, which ran out into the open sea.

"We got like, 10 minutes. We should get going. I'm gonna take a leak..."

"Yeah..."

Pedro was informative.

She, still sitting, unabashedly removed her left breast from the sweater and brought the baby to it. The baby quieted, though it hadn't made much sound. It had not been screaming for nourishment. This was a gift to it, her milk, her essence for her child. My throat was more parched than ever... I could scarcely breathe... couldn't speak...

I too, was still hungry. The burger, the fries, they were empty offerings. It wasn't them my stomach had been after, no, that was clear to me now. I needed to sate my loneliness, my true hunger. I wanted to take that child's place, shove it out of the way. Controversial thoughts clouded my brain, little fish up from the riverbed to pick through the debris, rip off chunks of leafy flesh and leave only the exposed bark, the damp wood to roll on down the stream... into the deep of the ocean...

My eyes surveyed her perimeters. Every inch was found by my ocular espionage, and if only my lips could describe what my eyes had seen. If only my lips could taste what my eyes made them thirsty for...

"Let's go man. We'll be late for SPORTING EVENT/MOVIE."

Pedro was right.

The adventure here was over, the debris failing on its quest, sinking to nestle in the depths of the riverbed. To sleep with the fishes.

Ten

Words

"**G**AH."

This is not a word, but it had suited my mood.

Earlier in the day I had given my hastily written story to Dirk. As he toddled off to read it, I became somewhat self-destructive for a period of about 2 hours, sinking into some half-assed post-partum depression. While Dirk read, I retreated to the porch to consume tobacco and coffee at a higher than usual clip and, with pen and paper in hand, decided that I would torture a few words, lop some limbs from a few nouns and hold the heads of several verbs underwater for a while.

I began with the word 'useful'. I spelled it out correctly in the middle of the page in a careful script, prim and proper, the belle of the line-ruled ball:

useful

'Useful' felt quite at home there, I imagined, nestled snugly in the middle of its paper, feeling purposeful in its use and in its world. I however, was going to have none of this jovial page-loving fun. Carefully, with my scalpel-pen, I leaned down over the word and began to alter it, ever so slightly. I took the quivering nub and with one quick and vile little tick I nicked the artery of the word and rendered it stupid. With a simple line a partial lobotomy had been administered, leaving the word drenched in cold self-parody, a drooling duality. With one flick the word became a hillbilly stereotype with a slack-jawed, gap-toothed cringe of a face and a t-shirt that proclaims 'Genius at Work':

usefull

Any good application of torture must come with a slight reprieve. The victim must be made to believe that their tormenter can be benevolent just as easily as they can be cruel. In this way, the victim feels that if they do the right thing or say the right words, there will come a period of relief, and possibly, if all goes well, permanent relief. This is why, for no other reason than to instil a false sense of hope in my poor little word, I gently sculpted a new letter for it, one to make it think that I wasn't such a bad guy after all. And so, my victim briefly became:

usefully

It was time to prove that I meant business. I was the internet kid with an opinion. I was the internet kid who slowly aids in the mutilation of our written word until all that is left is phonetic pronunciation in the interest of getting the job done fast over getting the job done right. "U R Gonna Die," I wrote in the top margin, letting the word know that trouble was indeed brewing, that I wasn't just a lazy plastic surgeon, grafting two extra letters on at my own malpractice pace. This is when I dumped the poor word under water:

Water
Usefully

Laughter trickled from my lips, watching it thrash about on the page under the weight of all those moist letters. I knew that survival was hopeless, but I had to hand it to the word. 'Usefully', née 'useful', was indeed a survivor. The word itself survived as a whole and in death, it would still be correct; still have meaning. I wasn't about to let that happen, so I added an addendum, a hastily scraped together new appendage, all elbow and grease, no meat or meaning:

Water

Usefully

↑

Less

I had mutated the once beautiful and airy 'useful' into the grotesque and hideous 'uselessfully' that was still in the throes and thrashes of a mid-afternoon drowning. The word still seemed defiant however, still somehow stoic amidst the mutilation and imperilment. So I threw it to the crocodiles. After my scrawling and scribbling madly around of the rapidly crinkling piece of loose leaf, it ended up looking something like this:

CROCODILE

CROCODILE   CROCODILE

CROCODILE

Water

Usefully   CROCODILE

↑

Less

CROCODILE AQUAMAN   CROCODILE

CROCODILE

"Is Aquaman there to save the day?" Dirk had appeared in the doorway behind me. I coughed out a sickly plume at the surprise.

"Thank you... for that..." I sputtered.

"Sorry. Didn't mean to get you all heebie-jeebie." He studied the word picture for a moment. "What are you doing?"

"Torturing words."

"Feeling useless?" Dirk asked.

"A little."

"Why?"

My cigarette met its end against the cement of the stoop. "I don't know. I get this way sometimes after writing something, especially the first draft of something. I have a huge collection of these things."

"Do you have a name for them?"

"Not as such, no."

"Do they serve a purpose?"

"They're therapeutic I guess. It's a way of taking out some writerly frustrations on language itself. No purpose other than that."

"You should dig some of them out for me. I think they may be of some use... with the help of a photocopy device."

"You've got the binder full of my stuff. They're all in there."

"Well that makes it easier, doesn't it?"

Before I had a chance to protest he added, "I liked your story. Come on in, let's rap."

Coffee mug cradled in hand I allowed myself to be led within the nest of Danger to the kitchen where Dirk took a seat in front of a steaming mug of coffee and my story, scrawled on the page like jumbled English with a case of bed head.

Sitting across from Dirk I hunched my back and leaned into the table, my chin dangling above the smooth wooden mesa and threatening to drop. My eyes had a sag to them and I carried a frown so thick and full you'd think I'd just been forced to watch the first season of *Survivor* on DVD. Dirk grinned like an idiot.

"I take it you aren't a fan of your story?" he said, inhaling the steam from the mug and then exhaling a breath upon the inky rippled pond within his mug.

"I just... don't like being judged."

"I suppose you didn't take much away from our session yesterday?"

"At the poetry night?"

He nodded.

"It's kind of difficult to change a person's mentality in a single day," I said. "Let alone the two hour period we spent at Dave's."

"That may be the case, but that's why we're taking baby steps with this writing thing. You've let me read your binder, which I haven't got around to yet. That was good because you relinquished your control over your ideas and expressions. Next, we went to Dave's because you needed to be put at risk and you did indeed get the reaction you were expecting. That was supposed to be validating. Was it?"

My head quivered in something approximating a nod.

"There you go. And now, you're going to be criticized one to one. You'll get over this whole thing sooner or later, I'm just trying to make the best of our time. We don't have long together and that means our baby steps are going to be a little rushed. So no, I don't expect you to change overnight, but I do expect you to lighten up a bit and stop being so damn mopey."

A sigh sped out of me at top speed.

"There you go again with the goddamn sigh. I liked your story. I thought it was engaging, and I also could see how it might use some improvements..."

For the next hour or so, we discussed the story and its ins and outs. He left me with a few helpful editorial suggestions and asked that I redraft it at some point.

"You don't have to give me the rewrite or anything, I'm not trying to be Principal Dirk, but I would like you to see it through."

"YOU KNOW, I'VE ALWAYS thought about writing this one story," Soup said.

After a quick dinner consisting of chilli and a bun, I had headed for my bedroom early to avoid socializing. Dirk however, had other ideas and before I knew it, I was sitting in the living room where after briefly discussing the day's events, Soup had launched into a description of a story he's always wanted to get out on paper...

We were gathered around the coffee table in the evening. Soup was wearing a tweed jacket and had a tobacco pipe filled with honest to goodness tobacco in lieu of his usual puffery. Robert and Jimmy kept to the weed to my chagrin. Dirk actually sat in with us, legs akimbo on the floor with his head resting on his chin. He seemed like a casual observer, less of an active participant than a decorative statue outfitted with a listening device.

"So, it's like this," Soup began, leaning forward, the pipe in his left hand fuming while his right gesticulated emphatically that he was really serious about all of this. "The future, all right? That's where we set the scene. It doesn't matter what year it is, it just has to be a little later on in the timeline. There are technological marvels plastered on every billboard, hover cars gliding silently down magnetic streets, you know, that kind of crap.

"The only problem with this future world is that humanity sucks. It seems that the majority of human beings are content to live lives of greed and avarice and sloth while there are a few planetary participants who feel that we as a species need to change. Things have become so bad and people on the whole have become so lazy and self-absorbed that when bombs start going off and mysterious infections start happening, no one cares enough to seek help or care about their fellow man."

"Sounds like the way things are now," coughed Jimmy, perm-a-smile sewn into his head until his creases had become so apparent he looked like a soft Dali portrait complete with fried bacon.

Soup rolled his eyes and continued. "So there's this group of four guys, right? They belong to a small group of human beings that still gives a flying fuck about the planet and they also happen to be really smart cats; these guys are right on the ball. They're all part of a scientific organization or something and they've been working on a time machine that is nearing perfection. These four guys have been tasked with the objective of going back in time and planting the seeds that will hopefully solve humanity's present woes."

"Future woes," Robert corrected.

"Whatever. You know what I mean. So, finally, these guys perfect this machine and they all go back in time. The plan is, they are going to head to a rural place outside of a major metropolitan area around three thousand years in the past…"

Robert snorted. "There were major metropolitan areas three thousand years ago?"

"Yeah, there damn well were," argued Soup. "I would call wherever the largest group of people decided to set up shop a major metropolitan area if there was a good enough ratio of townies to hillbillies."

"O-*kay*…" Robert snorted.

"Fuck, I can never just tell a story, can I? Always has to be fucking interruptions."

Dirk cleared his throat from his lotus stance on the rug. "So they traveled back in time to a rural area near a city?"

It was Soup's turn to snort. "So they go back in time and they find this couple, these two people wandering through the desert."

"Uh-oh," said Jimmy. "You can't be serious."

"Yeah! Joseph and Mary. These guys are going to create a miracle baby and build up a tragic life story for this boy so that they can scare the people of the future into being more moral and decent people!"

"That is the most blasphemous thing I've ever heard. You're telling me that, in your story, time travelling weirdo scientists leave a dystopian future to artificially inseminate a woman in order to pretend the boy is a messiah and preach goodness onto humankind therefore scaring the people of the future into being better people?" Jimmy took in a huge breath once the final words had left him. "That is ludicrous. You'd be crucified yourself for printing such insidious things."

"Would not," countered Soup. "It's perfectly acceptable to present a science fiction story centered around supposedly true events."

"You're a douche bag," Robert said. He was pointing angrily at Soup and causing the veins in his hand and his forehead to dance rhythmically as if strobe lights pulsed within his body to the tune of bad techno. "It's not just that your idea is bad, it's that it's the kind of thing that people do to get media coverage. *Oooh, look at me, I think that major religions are stupid and here's my angry story to illustrate what a media whore I am.* I thought you were above that kind of crap, buddy."

"I am," said Soup. "That's why I've never bothered to write it."

"No one would buy it anyway," said Jimmy.

"Yes they would," Robert barked, turning his angry disco-blood finger on Jimmy. "The same reason you'd want to publish something like that is that same reason a publisher would. Controversy means sales and sales means sequels and media coverage and publicity from all angles. If they want to burn your book, they have to buy hundreds of copies first so that they'll have something to burn."

"You never even let me get to the ending! That's the good part!" Soup puffed away on his pipe and spoke through clenched teeth and a self satisfied smirk.

"Oh, what's the fucking ending? They kill Jesus? *Har har*."

"Well, yeah, they kill Jesus, but then they go back."

"Back to the future?" I asked, daring to say anything at all.

"Yeah," Soup continued, "back to the future. They do what they set out to do, create their messiah, perpetuate his miracles and get back in their time machine with eager anticipation. They go back with high hopes that all of their problems will be solved and that they'll live happily ever after for the rest of their lives..."

"And...?" Jimmy asked absentmindedly while trying to re-light his joint. Robert had been holding it during his mini-diatribe and had let it die due to lack of interest.

"And everything is way, *way*, worse."

Jimmy briefly gave up with the lighter. "That's it? You tack some lame *Twilight Zone* ending on and call it a day?"

"It's a political statement," argued a defiant Soup. "It's supposed to be about how religion only makes things harder in life."

These guys were intolerable.

"You don't need to spell it out in some stupid Sci-Fi *Outer Limits* bullshit," spat Robert. "All you have to do is read the newspaper on a regular basis to see that. Why don't you just have your story be about some guys that read the newspaper and then come to the conclusion that religion is bad? That's a hell of a more interesting story than your contrived little wing ding."

"It's not contrived! And besides, I'm not going to write it, because as I said, I'm not too keen on inviting that kind of controversy into my life."

"Well," I said, "you could always use a pseudonym."

"You're an idiot too," Robert said, as if slamming a door.

"I've got a better story anyway," said Jimmy, who had successfully relit his joint and squinted happily as he spoke. "I got a better story than that one for sure."

"It can't help but be better than that one." Robert was trying to grab the joint away from Jimmy again, but after just having reignited the thing, Jimmy wasn't about to give it up.

"I thought of it while I was smoking."

"Weed?" Dirk asked.

"Yeah. So?"

"No reason."

Soup rejoined the conversation, happy that the topic had shifted from him. "Let the man speak. Jimmy, lay it on us man."

After pulling off a French Inhale, Jimmy began.

"So, there's this guy in a room."

"What kind of room?" Soup asked.

"I'm getting to that. Shhhh. It's a white room. Completely white. There are no windows, no pictures, no nothing. There is a door, also white, on the far end of the room. And this guy, he wakes up to discover that he's in this room. He's naked…"

"Was this one of your dreams?" Robert jibed, ever the asshole.

"Nah man, I read it in your diary."

Robert smacked Jimmy in the head.

"You're a real dick you know that?" Soup said.

"Yeah man. That's my only head, you know."

Dirk snickered. "And you keep filling it with that shit." he said, nodding towards the joint.

"Look, I'm just going to tell this thing, all right?"

There was a silent agreement that this should be so.

"Good. So, naked guy wakes up in white room. He's kind of a blank slate. He has no idea how he came to be in this room, who he is or where he is. He notices the door. He gets up and he tries to walk towards the door, but with each step he takes, the door gets further and further away. The crazy thing is, when he turns around, he is always the same distance from the walls as he was when he started walking. It's like he cannot reach the door at all to let himself out."

"So the door gets farther and farther away, but he stays in the same spot?" Soup seemed to be getting engaged.

"Yeah man. So the guy starts wondering, 'How did I get to be here?' He thinks that if there's a door and walls than the room must have been constructed, which means that someone built this room and put him there."

"Is this another god thing?" Robert said, flexing his arm unconsciously.

Jimmy, realizing that his joint had gone out again and was a lost cause, put the roach into the astray and said 'Yes, but it's not like Soup's fucking thing. Cool your jets."

"I will keep on slapping..."

"Calm the fuck down and let the man talk." Soup was getting agitated. "I want to hear the story."

Robert shrugged and sat back.

Jimmy went on. "This guy thinks that he must have done something wrong to be put in the room. He thinks that since he cannot reach the door, he must be being punished for something. This has him worried because he cannot remember what he had done to be punished. He thinks that he must have to please the person that put him in the room somehow in order to be let out.

"The guy looks around and there is nothing he can see that he may be able to use to prove his worth or atone for whatever it is that he did. He figures that he can only do one of two things. He must either work himself to the point of exhaustion or meditate and show that he can be submissive and thoughtful. It is at this point that he realizes something really, really bad. With every clean breath of air that he takes in, he's breathing out thick black smoke."

"How did he not notice that right away?"

Jimmy sighed. "I don't know. It's not important. It's only important that with every breath this guy takes, the room is getting more and more smoke-filled and less and less air-filled."

"Fine. Go on."

"The guy tries first to wear himself out from working hard. He runs in circles, tries to do push ups, jumps as high as he can into the air. He says out loud 'Look how I toil for you! Please let me out of here!' but there is no response. Now that he's breathing harder from so much exertion, the room is filling up with smoke faster, all billowing along the ceiling and working its way down to the floor. He decides he'll try and meditate; be calm.

"The guy lays down on the floor and tries to control his breathing. He tries to think about soothing things, but his mind keeps coming back to what will happen to him if he doesn't appease his captors. He will surely die in this room. He wonders if anyone knows that he is trapped here. He wonders if he has any family or friends that may be looking for him; if there is anyone else alive that knows that he exists? Suddenly, he becomes terrified. What if no one but him knows that he exists? If he is the only one aware of his existence, then his whole life has been meaningless.

"The guy can't think calm thoughts. He keeps coming back to the fact that he may die without ever being known by anyone at all. He gets up from his meditation, frantic. He's got to leave some kind of mark, some way that people will know that he existed. He sees nothing at all that can help him, and then he gets an idea. Maybe he can scratch a message into the wall.

"He goes to the wall and starts tearing at it with his fingers. He's not getting anywhere and he scratches harder and harder, breathing heavier and coughing as he begins to breathe smoke back into his lungs rather than air. He scratches at the wall so frantic and hard that he breaks off his nail and begins to bleed."

"That's gross man. Nails creep me out." said Soup.

"Oh it gets better than that. After his nail comes off and he notices the smear of blood on the wall, he gets an idea. He's going to build himself a pen. He takes his index finger of his right hand and places the tip of it into his mouth. He bites down, pushing past the pain until he severs the tip right off and goes to work writing his message on the wall."

I shuddered considering how much that would hurt. Surveying the room, this seemed to be the general consensus.

"What did he write?" Dirk asked.

"He wrote 'I was here'. And then, he died."

"You know, that's not bad." Soup said.

"It's a fuck of a lot better than that trash you were spewing." Robert grunted.

"Yeah, fuck you too."

"We all just want to be remembered. Just want to leave our mark." Jimmy said.

And with that, the room quieted in a thoughtful, though depressing way and it was not long before we all dispersed to bed.

Eleven

The Pigeon or the Egg

"**I** HAVE NO IDEA WHERE he is."

Soup was alone in the living room, reading the paper. Apparently he had the day off work. I'd spent the morning a little lost due to the fact that Dirk seemed to have gone missing. He had prepared my breakfast for the first three days I'd been here and now, I had crawled from sleep to find that there were no sausages quaintly wrapped in any form of bacon, there were no eggs and there was no coffee. Well, actually, all of these things *were* in fact present in their kitchen nooks and crannies, but damned if I had the initiative or skill to attempt their preparation. Upon opening the fridge to pull out the eggs, the carton seemed to be staring at me with contempt, mocking me, daring me to break them.

"C'mon," the eggs jibed, "you think you're hot shit, so why don't you do something about it?"

"Oh, I plan to!" I said.

"Yeah, right, as soon as you stop sucking on Dirk's tit you'll head on over and make us crack, right? You feelin' a little parched, not suckling on his chest right now, don'cha? You pussy."

"All right, listen here, *egg*. I can and will crack the living hell out of you if you don't shut up this instant."

"Right, right. No seriously, we believe you. Hey, lookit: this here's our best before date. We got a whole month yet to take you on. And if Dirk never comes back? Well, I figure we can both see how that'll end. You'll starve like the fucking whelp you are. Isn't that right, Bacon?"

"Amen," said the bacon, who had no right to get into this.

I shut the fridge and decided to make coffee. How badly could that go?

With a mildly successful pot of coffee under my wing, I smoked three cigarettes out on the porch and came back inside to find that Soup and Soup alone remained, calmly reading the paper and drinking a cup of my freshly made attempt at coffee.

"He must've left early this morning. Dirk'll do that sometimes. He goes away for weeks at a time. Sometimes he gets restless." Soup took a swig. "This is disgusting," he said.

"Yeah, I really don't have a clue sometimes." I muttered, half to myself.

"It's *coffee*," stressed Soup.

"Nearly."

"*Touché.*"

Of the three associates, I'd felt Soup was the most down to earth. He seemed the kindest of the three, with Jimmy being indifferent with a touch of crass and Rob being an absolute bastard. Taking a seat, the sofa dug into my back. A loose something prodded at my spine. I let it.

"What's the plan for today?" I asked of Soup, who somewhat ignored me as he perused the paper.

"You know, we really need to stop lying to ourselves," he said.

"What do you mean?" The cold anger in his voice put me off and the spine stinging something made me determined to endure.

"This global warming crap."

I let out a sigh of relief. Not the confrontation I had expected after all.

"What are you sighing about?"

"Nothing. Why?"

A cocked eyebrow suspiciously cast my way held firm as he folded the paper and set it on the table, reaching out for his mug of nearly-coffee. "This global warming debate really gets under my skin. Doesn't it bother you?"

I couldn't even feed myself. What did I care about global warming?

"I guess it's something of a tragedy..." I tried.

"You know, that word pisses me off too. 'Tragedy'. We throw that around like mad. A hurricane decimating an entire city isn't a tragedy. A guy losing all of his money and his house because of a fire isn't a tragedy. It's life. *Hamlet* is a tragedy.

"Anyway, this global warming thing aggravates me to no end. I don't understand it one bit."

"Well, it's a serious problem isn't it? I mean, if people are causing the destruction of the world, then we should do what we can to stop it, right?"

"Well sure," he said, recoiling slightly after another sip. "The thing is, the reasons we think we should be helping are lies."

I took a sip of the stuff myself. It really wasn't as bad as his face made it seem. "What reasons? Saving the planet?"

"Yeah, exactly. That's the lie right there. We don't care about the planet. We don't. I guarantee it. People as a whole might say that they do, but on an individual level, people only do what is in their self-interest. That's why we are causing global warming in the first place. 'What do you mean I can't drive my Hummer? It makes me feel safe'," this last bit was delivered with his chest puffed out and a strange drawl that made the words sound mentally challenged.

"I don't think that people do that," I said.

"Then you're naïve, Cheesebomb."

"Seriously, can you stop with the 'Cheesebomb'?"

"You think I like being called 'Soup'?"

"Why are you called 'Soup' anyway?"

"I used to work in the soup kitchen. Downtown. For the homeless. It's how I met these guys. I fed them and they called me 'Soup'."

"They were homeless?"

"Yup. Me too."

"And Dirk?"

Soup nodded. "Dirk was a liar, though."

This had taken an interesting turn. "What do you mean he 'was a liar'?"

"I'll leave that for him to tell you. Don't ask. It's not my place. He'll tell you eventually. It's his story, so he likes to spread it. He tells it better than I do anyway."

I was dumbfounded. I opened my mouth to say something, but the thoughts and words died on the tip of my tongue, each one executed as it attempted escape, shot down by some gingivitis sniper hiding in one of my cavities.

"The thing that really pisses me off about global warming," Soup reiterated as if to kill the sudden awkward silence, "is that no one really cares about the planet. People care about themselves. They keep being bombarded with all of this media that is telling them that global warming is going to cause serious harm to all of us very soon and it's getting to their heads. So Joe everyman feels like he's saving his own life when he goes to the grocery store and refuses a bag. It's ridiculous."

"Yeah, plus it would put all of those plastic bag manufacturers out of business. Think of all the lost jobs..."

Soup chuckled. "Cheesebomb scores a hit."

"I really don't think that that's what goes through someone's head when they refuse a bag..." I went on.

"Maybe not that exact thought, no. The delusional thing is that not only are we selfish creatures, we are so egocentric that we actually believe these small things make a difference. We'll refuse the bag, but we'll drive to the store. We'll recycle our bottles and cans but we'll buy hairspray and cosmetics that are made in a factory somewhere. We are deluding ourselves into thinking we can effect change by ignoring big issues and focusing on stupid little details. Seriously, I think that the plastic bag is like a martyr for the climate change cause."

"What happened to every little bit helps?" I asked.

"Every little bit only helps when you do every single little bit that you can. That's the idea. If you save one penny, but spend the rest, a penny saved is not a penny earned."

"Maybe it just starts small. Maybe people start with the bags, and then move on to driving less, or buying a hybrid car, or..."

"No. It doesn't work that way. Well, maybe in the rare case. The unfortunate thing is that the bag saver will think that's enough. They are doing their part. That's not even the biggest delusion though. You know what the biggest delusion is?"

I shrugged and sipped my coffee. I was picturing Soup standing on the street in rags, orating on top of a soap box about the End of Days.

"We actually seem to think that we are in control of the planet. We feel that we have the ability to control our Earth. That's the biggest delusion. I tell you my friend, there will come a time when people will be a long forgotten species and the Earth will be standing firm. When it's had enough of our destructive self imploding ways it'll shake us off like fleas."

"Isn't that a tad *cliché*?" I asked.

"It's the truth, my friend. There was a time when the average lifespan of a person was about forty years. We've managed to double that and now one in two people contract some form of cancer. I don't think that's a coincidence at all. I think that's nature's way of asserting who's really in control. We don't own our planet as so many hippie slogans would have you believe. We live in it, we pollute it and we will die because we don't learn from our mistakes. The world however, will soldier on." Soup sat back, mug in hand and waited for me to agree with him.

"You know," I said, "I think I'm gonna go for a walk."

MENACING CLOUDY FISTS SHOOK hard at me as I moved along the sidewalk forgetting to smoke the lit cigarette in my hand. The local strip mall loomed. There was a coffee place there that had good lattes. I would smoke and drink coffee and pretend like I was an everyday, honest-to-goodness human being that was on his morning coffee break, a reprieve from the daily grind that put food on his table and gave his life meaning. My fellow strangers would have no idea that they were looking at what was essentially a human failure on display for all to see, a mask of gleaming porcelain covering my hideous face.

The coffee shop was full of teenaged hippies whom I've never understood. In high school, I had dated one such '*nouveaux* hippie', a girl whose parents had been the real deal. I'd met them once, over at her house for dinner, practicing the meet-the-folks routine that we'd all have to dance later in life, over and over again. They had prepared spaghetti, probably as a cruel joke, to see their daughter's little crush try to politely eat the sloppiest food known to man. The whole thing was surreal. They actually had tie-dyed pieces of cloth strung up over their walls, great big testaments to an age long past, each one hanging just a little too close to floor lamps covered with fake gilding, turning the massive sunbursts into potential fire hazards. The living room played out like one big LSD trip, filled with enough colour to make a box of crayons seem dull by comparison. If it was what you dug on you could well indeed become addicted to a space like that, whether it was the love of the vibrant color of reminiscence or simply the feeling like you were in some otherworldly freak show. There was a pair of tiny bongo drums sitting on the table and an acoustic guitar in the corner. An ashtray in the center of the room, on the floor, held a tiny pair of roach clips. Over the course of the evening, her parents smoked up with their daughter several times, each time trying to pass the joint to me and each time having it politely passed to the next person in the weird little legs akimbo Pow-Wow circle we had formed on the floor. This was after dinner, after the laughter of my attempts at polite spaghetti had been forgotten, after they had let a glob of sauce and parmesan cheese remain on my nose for just long enough to bring them to giddy hysterics. This weed circle, in which they let their child partake, seemed to me the antithesis of what hippies had ever stood for. They weren't fighting any power, they weren't expressing free love, they weren't sticking it to any *man*. All I saw was stoners and bad parenting coupled with a desire for past glory with no means or ambition whatsoever to try and reclaim it. At the point where I could feel a buzz from all of the second-hand smoke filling the room, I excused myself from the circle just as the bongo drums came out and left the house to the giggles of the family and the rattling pat-a-pat-pat of badly played animal skins strung oh-so tightly and hypocritically over the wooden frames of their instruments of free expression. My relationship with the girl was over that day.

The other reason I don't get hippies is, because of the ways and messages that they preach, I constantly feel like I'm being judged. I feel like they don't want me around because I'm not worthy to be on Gaia's great planet with them. Maybe it's just me, but I feel like their eyes are those of a horror film portrait; fake smiles and a happy appearance plastered on forever while sinister eyes follow you around the room, or the hallway, leaving you just unsettled enough to get out of there.

So I paid for my coffee and fled the tie-dyed eyes and dreaded locks of hair and worked my way around the corner to suck on my latte and pretend I was competent.

The bench I ended up on was in an alcove surrounded on all sides by one-way windows. Only those within the building could see out into the world. I was putting myself on display in an open interrogation room. Those passing by in the halls or sitting in the offices on the other side of those windows would see me, proudly drinking coffee I could afford to buy and cigarettes that I could afford to smoke because Pretend Me could hold down a job and Pretend Me could spend his money like water and use it any way he saw fit.

As I proudly lied and puffed my way through mid-morning, I realized that I was not alone. There was something else here in the alcove with me. I had appeared in the corner of my eye, a tiny flutter of movement, white and thin that flecked across my vision as smoke wisped an curled around my face, mingling with the steam from my latte in a casual, poisonous dance.

Turning my head slightly I could see a pigeon, wings fluttering, facing the window in one of the corners. The bird looked ragged and torn, its wings moving like flailing broken appendages, and its feathers missing in places as if it had been in one fight too many. The bird opened its mouth at the window and hissed. It was like no sound I'd ever heard a pigeon make, unfamiliar enough for me to think that it might not be a pigeon after all. The bird was making this hideous sound at its own reflection, pausing now and again to peck at its mirror image in vain, tiny clicking sounds as beak struck glass.

I moved closer to it. The bird noticed my presence but seemed largely unfazed. A human was insignificant right now. This bird was having a crisis.

With wild eyes, the pigeon glared and strutted around, its sight trained on the strange nemesis in the glass. With jagged, tired movements the poor thing fought itself like a prize fighter who'd met its equal, each blow met by the same blow, striking the glass, each bird moving in exactly the same pattern of territorial pissing, wanting the other one gone.

"It's you," I said.

The bird ignored me and kept at it, fighting itself with great determination, struggling to take care of this intruder.

"You can't beat it. It's you, don't you get it? You leave, it's gone. Find a new spot." I got up and moved even closer, the bird sidling away from me further along the wall of glass, watching with a keen eye as its reflected intruder kept pace with it. I sat back down.

"Stupid bird," I muttered to myself. The thing looked so ragged and pathetic, so caught up in a futile struggle I wondered if it had been eating anything. "Stay right there, you idiot. I'm going to get you some grub."

I got up and returned to the coffee shop and approached the counter. The clerk, sporting a genuinely cheery smile asked what she could do for me.

"There's this bird out there, in the alcove," I explained. "I think it might be hurt and I was wondering if you had anything that a bird might like to eat... you know... like seeds or... something."

"Uh..." said the clerk.

A particularly greasy hippie kid approached me at the counter. "That bird at the window?"

"Yeah."

"We have mixed nuts and berries," said the clerk. "Sort of a trail mix..."

"That bird is intense," said the hippie.

"Mixed nuts and berries it is," I said, and then to the hippie, "Intense?"

"Yeah man, that bird is right into his thing. He's been there for days. He won't let it go. He just keeps pecking at himself like that. He's so *driven*."

"Three-fifty," said the clerk.

"Seriously? For nuts?" I asked incredulously.

The clerk nodded.

"Yeah man, that bird is so motivated. He's been consumed by his own reflection, but not, like, in love with it... he wants to kill himself and he doesn't even know it. We watch him for a bit in the morning. Past few days that's all he's done."

"That's not what I'd call motivation," I said, reluctantly paying the uncaring clerk and taking my all together too small packet of nuts from her bony little fingers. "That's what I'd call suicidal."

"No way. He doesn't know any better. He's protecting his territory."

"No, he's slowly dying. Now, if you'll excuse me, I'm going to go and feed him."

I left to the hippie's cry of "Suit yourself!" and headed back to my alcove. For some reason the thought of the hippie kid tossing a hacky-sack at the poor bird's head while his chums giggled crept into my mind. If that was how this bird had lost even one feather, I'd shave the damn kid's dreads right off and force feed them to the mother-fucker.

The bird was where I had left it, still gnawing at the window bird who gnawed right back. I opened the bag of fruit and nuts and took out a handful.

"All right now bird," I said, "This food cost me more than I ever thought I'd spend on a handful of nuts, so you better enjoy it."

The food flew out from my hand, surrounding the pigeon on all sides with what must have been the caviar of granola. The bird leapt to the side to avoid being hit by the falling bits, but it did not make a move to eat a single nut. It hopped further away from the food and kept right on pecking as its reflection continued to retaliate.

"You have to eat this!" I yelled at it. "You will die if you don't eat. That's just you in the mirror!" I let fly another loose handful of nuts. Still the bird persisted in ignoring me. It moved further down, still strafing the window to keep its eye trained on the sinister interloper from the netherworld.

My nuts had attracted another pigeon. This new bird swooped down and started gobbling down all of the seeds strewn about the ground.

"Get out of here! Shoo! Those aren't for you!" I waved my arms at the new bird causing it to fly briefly into the air, touching down a little further on. It moved towards the nuts once again but stopped this time to peck at the pigeon still intent on murdering its reflection. The new bird let its beak dig into its dazed brethren, burying its face into the back of the poor confused creature. The confused animal did nothing. It let itself be pecked at and attacked, made no move to defend itself, simply allowing the meat to be torn into all along its back and neck. Only its reflection mattered.

"Get out of here, you bastard!" I yelled at the interloper. I got up and rushed at both of the birds. The new bird fled in terror. The old bird, the first bird, my bird, did nothing but strafe the window and keep on the offensive.

I slunk back to my place on the bench, becoming frustrated enough that, without thinking, I balled the bag of nuts into my fist and hurled it at the window. It struck right next to the bird, scaring it slightly, but not enough to distract it as the nuts and fruit chunks rained down over its body and its image in the glass took the same shrapnel with the same uncaring glaze in its eye.

"You fucking stupid bird! This is no time for an existential crisis! Your life is in jeopardy!"

I realized that I was crying. I wiped my eyes with the back of my hand and stared bleakly at my own reflection.

"Fuck you," I said.

To whom, I'm not exactly sure.

Twelve

Lesson 3:
A Distinct Lack of Femininity

"WHAT'S THIS?" I ASKED looking at the piece of paper Dirk had handed me. It was a stupid question, because it was clearly my résumé. It was no résumé of anything I had ever in my life accomplished, but it was definitely mine. My name was across the top in professional typeface, underlined and italicized, as if my name had somewhere to go and it needed to be there *now*, racing across the page. Beneath it lay a list of accomplishments from someone else's life, or just whatever life Dirk had decided would suit me. Under the education listing it said that I had completed a typing and bookkeeping course and could type one hundred and thirty words per minute. I had also completed some college. Under the work experience header, I had been employed at a restaurant I had never heard of — "Calamity's" — for three years until it folded. After that, I'd worked at the zoo as a beekeeper, and as my reason for leaving Dirk wrote "Unsatisfactory Ointment Supply". Once my stint as an apiary apprentice had sorely ended, I had, apparently, most recently worked as a waiter in a small hotel restaurant. Under my reason for leaving:

"Butter Incident — More Information Upon Request". I had also been a volunteer at a pet shelter for most of my life due to my profound love of pugs, and my hobbies included writing, softball and matching cheese to the correct vintage and variety of wines.

"It's your résumé, genius," was Dirk's reply.

We were in the car on our way to God knows where. Dirk was keeping things a secret as usual. He had told me to dress as he put it, "Like I meant it," which I gathered to mean dress pants, shirt and tie and had handed me the résumé about ten minutes into our drive with a big goofy smile stretched across his impish face.

"Well, it's got my name on it, sure..."

"And your many accomplishments!"

"I don't like pugs or bees."

"You don't like pugs?"

"No. They're hideous little beasts. Faces like mouldy deli meat with a breathing problem."

"I think it's a given that mouldy deli meat has a breathing problem."

Sighing loudly, with a slight groan I pretended to study the ridiculous piece of paper.

"There you go sighing again," said Dirk. "I used to have a pug. They're quite friendly."

"I will sigh if I want. Why *bees* of all things?"

"I tried to pick interesting things that no one would care to follow up on. Who's going to go to the trouble of calling the zoo, asking to be put through to the Bee Manager and ask questions about a former employee? What does a bee have to do with any other job... ever?"

"Why didn't you just get me to make my own résumé?" I asked.

"Because you'd have fucked it up. Also, from what you've told me, you don't want any of your references checked anyway. Look, I tried to keep it simple. You've more or less only worked in restaurants your whole life, so I stuck two on there. That way if you get asked any questions about those restaurant jobs, you'll have something to fall back on."

"What is 'Calamity's'? I've never heard of it."

"Not surprising. Never existed. It folded, no reference to check. I win!"

"What about this hotel job? They could check that one?"

"I know someone that works at that hotel. I've already given them a 'heads up'. You'll get a glowing reference. It won't be necessary though. We've got nothing to worry about."

"And why is that?" I asked.

"Because you won't need it. I just made up the résumé so that I could circulate it over the last few days to a few choice places. That's why I've been missing for two days. I was preparing us for lesson three."

"Which is?"

Dirk looked over at me while pulling to a stop at a red. "Learning when to keep your mouth shut and being thankful for the help you get from others. Well, that's it in a nutshell anyway.

"I have had issues my whole life with people giving me a hand. I've hated it. I've always tried to do everything myself and be proud that I didn't have to ask anybody for help. And you know what? It's bullshit with a capital *shit*. Be thankful you have people that care about you. I realize that you accepting my help in the first place is a great first step for you, but you could live at my house for years and not learn to appreciate the help of others. So, in the spirit of give and take, I'm going to use my suave savvy to get you a job and you are going to use whatever skill you have to keep it and make some actual money."

"So we're on our way to a job interview?" I asked.

"That's the one, Cheesebomb. That's the one."

"Do zoos even have bees?"

"Shut up."

THE REASON DIRK HAD written on the phony résumé that I'd been a typist was the same reason he'd told me to dress respectably. He was going to try and get me a job with a small accounting firm as their secretary. Dirk himself had dressed more than respectably. He was wearing the 'Regis Combo': black pants, black shirt, black tie and naturally, black shoes and socks.

"You look like a funeral director," I told him as we got out of his car in front of Alistair and Smythe, Chartered Accountants., a free standing old home that had been converted into an office in the heart of downtown. Ivy climbed the walls, carefully clipped back around the windows and the red brick of the old building could barely be discerned through all of the green.

"No," he said, "I look like your attorney."

"What?"

"I'm your legal counsel. I'm here to represent you in this interview."

"That's preposterous," I said. "Who's going to hire someone that brings their legal counsel to a job interview. They'll be too terrified to hire me!"

"Not from what I've gleaned. After I faxed off your résumé on Monday morning, I received a call from three prospective jobs that same day, which I was certainly not expecting. The first one was a brusque fellow who after I told him that I was your representative almost immediately discontinued our conversation. The second played along but didn't set up an interview at all. This guy, however — whose name is Ron by the way — was very meek and mild and I was able to bully my way into an interview very easily. Then I went to the firm's website and found his picture. This guy is putty in our hands, believe me." Dirk stretched and straightened his tie. "Ready?"

Another sigh was my half-hearted reply.

"I'll take that as a 'yes'."

Dirk motioned for me to follow him up to the door of the building and, after giving himself a long shake, grabbed the knob, and with that we were shuttled into the foyer.

There was no one present to greet us at the reception desk, which was probably why Dirk had received a phone call so quickly. There was a bell on the reception desk with a tented piece of paper with a handwritten note reading "PLEASE RING FOR SERVICE" in an awkward scrawl. Dirk calmly approached the counter, raised his hand above the bell, looked back at me with a wink and a grin, and *DING*.

We stood in the foyer looking around impatiently for nearly ten minutes before Dirk rang the bell again. Still, no one came out to greet us.

"This will not do," said a suddenly very professional Danger, playing the part of the attorney quite competently. He stalked his way over to a closed door beside the reception desk, flung it open and called out, "Pardon me, but is there anyone available to speak with us? We're due for an appointment at two o'clock. A fellow named Ron?"

Suddenly, a plodding sound could be heard above us, groaning through the old wooden bones of this ancient house. The sound of heavy feet tumbled across the ceiling and made their way to the head of a staircase to the side of the reception desk. A portly fellow, balding and bespectacled ambled down the stairs in a thick waddle, his shirt and pants straining in great agony at being forced to stretch against the man's descending form. Dirk and I watched the man climb down, muttering to himself as he made each step as if walking through a sleeping field of coiled and venomous snakes. He touched down on our level and squinted up at us through his thick lenses.

"Ron?" Dirk asked him once he had seemed to regain his breath.

"Yes, that's me. How can I assist you?" the little man managed, breathing laboured breaths, air escaping his lungs as if fleeing the solitary confinement of a truly insidious POW camp.

"We are your two o'clock," Dirk explained. "I spoke to you on the phone on Monday. I represent my client here, the man looking for the receptionist position."

Ron gave me a tepid and curious up and down look.

"To be honest," Ron said, "I had been expecting a... uh..."

"A woman?" Dirk finished for him. "I realize that his name is a little androgynous, but I assure you, my client is anything but feminine."

The bastard. Dirk had known full well that all of the employers would naturally assume I was female since I was applying for the position of a secretary.

"Uh... well..." tried Ron.

"Yes, well you see, that's exactly why I'm here." Dirk offered his hand for a shake. "Name's Demeter Quail, I'm a private attorney."

Ron held out his stupefied hand as his stupefied mouth uttered, "Huh?"

"Ronnie, my good man," Dirk began, vigorously shaking Ron's hand and asserting which side of the desk the pants would be worn in this interview, "my client here feels that it is necessary to have me on as council for this opportunity for employment because, well... do you have somewhere we can sit and talk? I'd prefer some table time with you my good man."

"Uh... yes," Ron said, yanking his hand away a bit too quickly from their prolonged shake. It seemed he'd been afraid Dirk might decide to keep it.

"Please, lead the way."

Dirk walked behind Ron with purpose. His footfalls came a little too hard, each one ricocheting off the thin wooden walls and getting lost within the hollow plaster. The corridor Ron led us down was through the door Dirk had first poked his head through. It was lit in a thick yellow that glommed onto the red paint of the walls and the ochre wainscoting. The whole thing felt very ancient. The realization that I knew the word 'wainscoting' troubled me.

Ron led us into a board room with a large round table. He took a seat at one end and I sat with Dirk at the other.

"Ron, before we go any further, I'd like to formally introduce my client." Dirk stood and motioned for me to follow. He exchanged our names and I took Ron's hand and gave it a little shake, firm but not nearly the crazed jackhammer of Dirk's madman handshake earlier. The portly fellow had a handshake that felt like runny JELL-O. In the moment of contact, my distaste of hand-sanitizer seemed foolish.

"Pleased to meet you," I said.

"Uh... likewise..." offered Ron.

"Ronnie... do you mind if I call you Ronnie?" Dirk asked. Ron opened his mouth, his tongue searching for the most polite way to do what his brain was telling him, when Dirk cut him off mid gape with, "Good then. Ronnie, my client here has an issue. Do you know what that might be? Can you hazard a guess?"

Ron tried again to form words to no avail.

"No?" Dirk resumed. "Well, my client has been searching long and hard for a job just like this one. A very long time wouldn't you say?" Dirk finished this thought by turning to me with eyebrows raised.

"Yes. Yes, I would say that," I replied.

"Good. I thought you might. See Ronnie, the thing of the matter is, despite the fact that he's applied several times and been interviewed for a miraculous one hundred percent of those applications, he's been turned down *every single time.* Now why do you think that might be Ronnie?"

"Well... uh... he's..."

"You hit the nail on the head that time Ronnie. '*He*' is exactly the problem. *He* is not a woman. That's the reason. What else could it be? *He*'s certainly qualified, wouldn't you agree?"

"Well..."

"Of course you agree, otherwise, we wouldn't *be* here, would we Ron?"

"No, I..."

"You suppose not. And you'd suppose correct. You're a smart guy Ron. I can see that in you. You're clearly a guy who's got his wits about him. You saw an opportunity in my client and you took it; wisely so. My client is an excellent individual. You'll be pleased with his performance."

"He is rather... inexperienced... at this sort of work, though," Ron said, finally breaking through Dirk's verbal barrier.

Dirk smirked at him and waggled his finger. Ron wiped his thick brow with the back of his hand, the moisture glistening off as he moved his hand beneath the table to, presumably, wipe off the sweat on his trousers. Dirk reclined in his chair. "Now isn't that the real issue here, Ronnie? Why do you suppose my client doesn't have any experience?"

"Because he's never done this sort of work before?"

"And *why* hasn't he done this sort of work before?"

"Because..."

"Of unfair gender bias, Ron, that's right. You see, Ron, I'm just here to ensure equality. You need a secretary. My qualified client needs a job. All I'm saying is, look past his lack of T-and-A and you'll find a hard working, diligent man with a lot to give. Don't you find it a bit unfair that his lack of experience didn't hold him back from an interview, but during the interview, with a total of three sets of male genitalia in the room it's suddenly an issue?"

"But..."

"But... ?"

Instead of continuing his thought, Ron paused with a quizzical look and asked, "T-and-A?"

"Tits and ass, my man. Come on, you knew that. Let's be frank here. We all know that a male client is going to be more inclined to do business somewhere if there's a bit of sex appeal to the place, right?"

Ron's head did something that could almost be considered a nod.

"Well any client is going to bring their business to a qualified, able and — above all — competent business regardless of its sex appeal, right? I mean, I'd get my insurance from Lloyd's of London over ING even if the secretary at ING was hotter... wouldn't you?"

"I'm not sure..."

"Really, Ron? That's too bad. I thought you were better than that. It's a sad situation when men in your position look for a trophy hire, don't you think?"

"Well, I don't think..."

"That's a shame Ron. I think too much sometimes. Keeps me up at night.

"Look, let's cut to the chase here. Ron, my client may not be the most attractive person on the planet. He may even look a bit... 'off' to tell you the truth. But there's one thing I know and know well, and that's the calibre of his personality.

This man is a winner. A sure-fire hit. If he were a movie, he'd smash box office records. If he were a golf pro, he'd hit nothing but aces. If he were a NASCAR, he wouldn't explode. He's a hardworking, diligent guy, has a good telephone voice, types quickly, and knows how to work a filing cabinet. The guy's practically a Swiss Army Knife, for crying out loud! The one thing he doesn't have is a vagina. Are we going to discount his worth over something so simple as a difference in sex?"

"Well, no, but..."

"Look, Ron, here's what I offer you:. a challenge. You seem like the kind of guy who like a good challenge, and that's what I'm going to give you. This man here, this brave and fearless crusader, wants to work for you. You give him the benefit of a two week probationary period, starting immediately, and I promise you'll want to keep him on. What do you say?"

Ron, flabbergasted, stared incredulously at Danger, then at me, mopping more sweat from his forehead and in the process, revealing the stains in his underarms from the nervous moisture. He opened his mouth once again and then... "Well... I suppose, we *could* give him a try... I mean... if he's as good as you say he is..."

"Oh he is," said Dirk. "He really is."

"Well... oh, all right. I'll give you your two weeks. I must say, having one's attorney present... this is as unorthodox a thing as I've ever encountered." Ron stood up and offered his hand for me to shake once again. After seeing how much sweat he was capable of producing I forced my face into a smooth and friendly smile, took his hand and said, "I really appreciate this. Honestly sir, you won't be disappointed."

"Well then, uh... I shall need your social insurance number and your identification tomorrow morning. You're well and good to start tomorrow?"

"Of course he is," Dirk said. "In fact, we'd very much prefer it."

"Well then... I shall see you tomorrow... uh... eight o'clock?"

"Certainly. I'll be here bright and early."

After all the final pleasantries had been exchanged, Dirk and I let ourselves out, went back into the hall and heard the unmistakable thump of a defeated man dropping into a comfy chair.

"What the hell just happened in there?" I asked quietly.

"Don't fuck this up, that's all I ask", he muttered

With that, 'Quail' and I made our way back to the car and drove off towards home with silly little shit eating grins.

Thirteen

Lesson 4:
Keeping it Interesting

"I THINK THAT WE HAVE time for one more lesson today. We'll do a 'send off' before you go to work."

We were eating breakfast for lunch, back at Dirk's house and high off of our recent victory at Alistair and Smythe, Chartered Accountants.

"And what, pray tell, is my big send off?"

"We will learn to keep things interesting."

"Then why," I asked, "are we once again eating sausage wrapped in a bacon?"

"Because it's tasty! That, and we should probably finish it all off before the meat goes bad."

"Well all right then."

Dirk's face changed suddenly and in the most bizarre way. Initially, he'd been sporting his I-know-something-you-don't-know grin. Once I'd said "Well all right then," and started chewing a bit of bacon I'd unwrapped from a sausage, Dirk's grin faded quickly and was replaced for a split second by a confused deer-in-the-headlights kind of open mouthed shock. This was immediately pushed aside and in its place there was a look of the kind produced by someone who's just made a breakthrough, a science lab outcast who would be proven right against the odds, goddamn it! Through all of the split second expression swapping he had been wagging his finger like a demented mime portraying a confused metronome.

"AHA!" he shouted and stood up so quickly that his chair toppled to the floor behind him like an awkward, boxy giraffe with rigor mortis. He stood wagging his finger in my face while I calmly chewed my tender, juicy bacon and stared limply at him. He kept at it, chuckling to himself until I finally gave up and shrugged.

"What?" I said, pausing mid chew.

"You did it! Or rather, you didn't do it!"

"Did didn't do what?"

"You are making progress my friend! You are moving beyond the defeatist mentality you had when we first met. You are starting to accept external forces and realize that the whole world isn't against you!"

I swallowed, put my fork down, took a sip of water. "What did I do?"

"You, my friend, didn't sigh!"

"So?"

"So you've been sighing at everything since the day I met you! Every time I try and take you somewhere as a surprise, you sigh, you put up a fuss, you mope and whatnot."

"I don't think that that's entirely true. I have done everything you've asked me to do. And to be honest, it is paying off. I've got a job, I'm doing a bit more writing, I mean, there's not a lot to complain about."

"Well, from the general consensus in the house when you first arrived here, we all thought you were a little mopey. You're changing my friend. And for the better. And that means that today's lesson couldn't come at a better time!"

"And today's lesson is about 'keeping things interesting'?"

"Yep! We're all about doldrums today. We're going to kick some serious doldrum ass."

"Well then let's get to it."

Dirk picked up his chair, set it back down and finished off the rest of his meal with a smile.

ONCE THE BREAKFAST FOR lunch dishes had been cleared and cleaned, I went out to the front porch for a smoke while Dirk organized whatever things we'd be needing today.

The wind was cool and clean on my face in the simmering sunlight as I thought about what The Danger had said about all of the sighing. I breathed deeply, cool clean air filling my lungs. The cigarette was forgotten as my spine slackened and a wave of relaxation overtook me.

As I was drifting away, Dirk burst from the house with a backpack, slammed the door shut behind him and locked the deadbolt with excited and sloppy fingers.

"Are you ready for awesome?"

"I suppose that I am."

"Then holy-o-fuck, let's get it on!"

Dirk began running full tilt down the sidewalk in the direction of the train. "What are you waiting for?" he called.

I threw down my butt and tried my best to catch up, losing Dirk pretty early into the race. I figured he'd be waiting for me at the train station with some idiot grin and a quip about how smokers are slow. When I got to the train station however, things were not as I had imagined them.

Dirk was crouched in a grouping of shrubs near the platform. As I approached he poked his head through a bush and waved me over. When I got near enough I could see that he was no longer wearing the T-shirt and jeans that he'd left the house in. He was now sporting a pair of swim trunks and nothing more. Well, almost nothing. He also had on a pair of flippers and was in the middle of pulling a snorkel and goggles out of the backpack when I got near enough to ask him, "What the hell are you doing?"

"Teaching you our lesson for the day. Come on, get into the shrubbery!"

I climbed inside.

"So, what are you doing?"

"This is how we met!"

"No, we met over the phone."

"Yes, but we met over the phone while I was keeping it interesting. I am a firm believer in the fact that, for the most part, people live very mundane lives. I like to jive it up a little, give them something to talk about at dinner or with their friends. I like to help them keep their lives interesting."

"I don't have to..."

"Wear flippers? No. Why? You didn't bring an extra set did you? No, you have a more important job."

"Which is?"

"To throw water on me every now and then."

He reached into the backpack and pulled out a 2-litre bottle of water.

"How did you fit all of that in there?" I asked him.

"That's of no consequence at the moment."

"No, really, it seems impossible. Is that bag like one of those clown cars?"

"Clown cars? Like Esperantos?"

"I think you mean El Caminos."

"No, I mean Esperantos. Those cars that are half car, half truck. Mullet mobiles. That's as close to a clown car as I can figure."

"Esperanto is a language."

"Says who."

"It is! It's a made up language."

"Did you make it up? Like, right now? To fuck with me?"

"No, some guy made it up."

"You're some guy."

"I didn't make it up!"

"Whatever. I'm not interested in speaking El Camino right now. I'm interested in making some lives a little livelier. Here."

Dirk pulled a small plastic cup out of the bag.

"This," he said, "must be filled with water which will then be thrown at me whenever I need it to be."

"How will I know when to throw it on you?"

"You'll know. I'll give a very clear indication. I may even say, 'Hey, throw some water on me!' You never know."

I took the cup from him and he shoved his regular clothing into the bag. He then donned the snorkel and goggles and stood up with purpose, marching out of the bush.

"Here we go..."

I followed Dirk out of the bush and immediately noticed the stares and laughter emanating from the passersby. Dirk bowed to them, and kept walking. He positioned himself at the foot of the staircase that led up to the train platform and waited for me to catch up. I stood beside him and set down the water.

"If you would, my good man, please fill a cup."

I opened up the bottle and filled the cup.

"Splash the first cup on me and then fill up another. Do it with a flourish, right in my face!"

I pulled back my arm and let fly, dousing the goggle encased head of my comrade and then bent down to refill the cup.

It was ten o'clock in the morning, past rush hour but the platform still teemed with people. Dirk stood like an explorer, holding a flattened hand above his eyes, surveying his territory. As I stood at the ready with my cup of water, he waited for people to come close to him and then:

"Excuse me? Random stranger?"

"Uh... yeah?"

"Could you tell me which way to the ocean?"

"There's no ocean anywhere near here."

"Well then I've been lied to."

"Someone told you there was an ocean here?"

"They most certainly did."

"This is some kind of joke right?"

"Are you laughing?"

"Uh..."

"I can see that you are not."

"Who's this guy?" This was a common question. They would point at me and ask this with a knowing smile, like they either enjoyed this farce or they though we were idiots. Probably a little of both.

Dirk would reply: "He's the liar."

"The liar?"

"Yeah, the guy that told me there was an ocean here."

"Then why are you standing with him?"

"He keeps me wet."

At this point, I would splash him again.

Once soaking wet, Dirk would say, "Have a beautiful day!" and the stranger would either return the sentiment and walk away or call us crazy and walk away. Either way, it was very entertaining.

Of course, not everyone was receptive. A good percentage of the walkers were in a hurry, not wanting to be bothered by two madmen when work was waiting. Others were insistent that they couldn't spare any change and some even threw change at our feet while they hurried past. If they did throw any change at us, Dirk would gather it up and hand it over to me.

"Keep this in your pocket. We'll need it later."

There was one guy in particular that didn't think that we were funny at all.

"Excuse me? Random stranger?"

The man was dressed in business attire and held a briefcase.

"Get a job," he said, and started to move on.

"You misunderstand sir!" Dirk called after him.

The guy stopped halfway up the staircase, turned around and came back down.

"Look, do me a favour and don't fucking talk to me. You people harass me twenty four seven. I get out the door and immediately, some guy asks me for a cigarette. I get downtown and I get bugged for change every five goddamn steps and now I have to talk to some fruit at the train station who's got some stupid fucking gimmick to bilk money out of honest, hardworking folks like me just trying to get through our goddamned day! So do me a favour and leave me the fuck alone! What do you say to that, huh?"

"I say that we are having light-hearted fun and that you are a prick."

"I said don't fucking talk to me!"

The guy was going way overboard. It seemed like he was taking out some personal vendetta against the homeless on us two screwballs trying to lighten up his day. He was about to launch into another rant when Dirk turned to me, grabbed the cup of water from my hand and threw it into the guy's face.

Dripping wet, arms held out at his sides and extreme hatred all over his face, the man exclaimed, "Why the fuck did you do that?"

"Because I don't think it can be construed as assault. Have a super day!"

I thought the guy was going to kill Dirk, leaving me to pick up loose shreds of Danger from the train platform. Instead, and inexplicably, the guy just walked off the way he had come, away from the platform, swearing about how late he was going to be. Dirk turned to me and shrugged. "Wanna get going?"

"He did kind of sour things up, didn't he?"

"A touch, yes."

"Did you not think he was going to beat the living fuck out of you?"

"I had a feeling he just needed to vent. Even if he needed to vent about what a callous buffoon he is. Speaking of which, how much money did we accidentally earn today?"

I dug into my pocket and pulled out the coins, holding them in my palm as I fingered them with my other hand.

"Three bucks and change."

"Not bad at all. We'll make up for his ignorance. Come on! I've got to change and then we're heading downtown!"

"What do you want to do with the water?"

"Well, dump the rest into the bushes and bring the bottle. It's an extra ten cents."

I poured out the remainder of the water and waited for Dirk to return from the bushes like some backwater superman. Once he'd changed back into his plainclothes he emerged out of the shrubs and took the bottle from me, placing it back into the bag.

"I'll just tuck this back into my Esperanto..."

"You're a dink Dirk."

We got up onto the platform and onto a train heading downtown.

Once seated, Dirk turned to me and said, "You know, I used to live on the streets."

"I know."

"You know?"

"Yeah. Soup told me. I asked him about his name and he said he used to volunteer in a soup kitchen. He said you were all homeless."

Dirk was quiet for a moment. "I wasn't homeless," he said. "I just lived on the streets."

The rest of the ride was taken in silence.

WE ARRIVED IN THE vertical sprawl of downtown at around noon. The streets were teeming with business types on their lunch breaks, tourists with their cameras and fanny-packs, and the odd ragged homeless person, hands outstretched and pleading with anyone within earshot.

Dirk immediately approached a group of these destitute individuals outside of a small park near the train station. The park was a commemorative affair, bedecked with monstrous bronze statues that heralded brotherhood and the generous founders of the city. It was the most ironic place for the downtrodden to congregate and hopefully, that's why they did so.

"Fellas!" Dirk grinned as he approached the group of men and the lone woman where they loitered against a cement façade covered with ivy and draped in the branches of trees that hung over the side of the wall from the park.

A tall man with long, scraggly gray hair and a thick white-shocked beard came forward. He was dressed in a dirty, rumpled coat in the style that cowboys wear, with the thick leather material and the slit down the back where the coat separates to facilitate horseback riding. The man was an urban cowboy without a horse or a home to call his own. There was a wizened way about him, nothing sinister dwelt within this man at all, and as we approached and said, "Well if it isn't Mr. Danger himself! What brings you down here today my boy?"

Dirk took the man's hand and pulled him in for a man hug. For the uninitiated, the man hug consists of a pseudo-handshake in which both participants lock hands and pull the other towards themselves. The men then wrap their free arm around one another and, with their other hand balled into a fist, pat each other on the back a couple of times before releasing their grips and letting go. This is the 'man hug'.

"What's shakin', Dirk?"

"I come with good tidings!"

Dirk introduced me around the group. Apparently he helped them out quite frequently. The cowboy was called Phil.

Dirk turned to me after we'd all been introduced. "Got that money?" he asked.

I dug it out of my pockets and handed it to him.

"It's not much today." He pulled a ten dollar bill from his pocket and handed that and the change over to Phil. "I've got this too," he added, pulling the bottle from his backpack. He tossed it to one of the men standing with Phil.

"Hey, 'not much' is all right with us."

"You guys share this, right?"

"You know it."

Dirk didn't say too much to the huddled group. The whole encounter seemed very strained and awkward. I began to envision a scenario:

Dirk, as a homeless man, knew this group. Maybe he was a part of this group. Him and the associates. They were all together under the same blanket sky, all vagrants begging for petty morsels from the more fortunate. With each and every passing day, they became more like a family, getting to know one another, sharing scraps and change and stories about how things used to be and about how things would get better.

Then, somehow, Dirk and the associates managed to get out of it all. Maybe they saved up a secret stash, maybe they all got jobs and tried their hardest to get out of the impossible lives they'd found themselves in. Maybe they made enough to start out with a room at the Y, saving scraps here and there. Dirk and the associates grew apart from this extended family over time and managed to move into a better place. All of this grew heavy on Dirk's conscience, that some of them had to be left behind. This, I imagined, was why he came here to do this. This was why we were here. A distant, troubled relationship with memories holding everything together.

I had noticed that the conversation had died off. Dirk was fumbling for words, something I had never seen him do.

"Look," he said, "we... we gotta go. You guys stay safe, all right?"

They all nodded in agreement and Dirk pulled me away. This was a guilty relief. I felt bad for being there in the first place. I felt like Howard Hughes, wanting to disinfect myself and flee from these wretches who didn't deserve to be thought of that way. I felt like a bigot and bully. And worst of all, I felt lucky. That was the guiltiest part of the whole experience. I had been whining my life away while others had reason to whine and did not. The cowboy, Phil, somehow maintained a certain dignity despite his situation and this was what made me feel, more than I've ever felt, like a lousy human being.

Once we were far enough away, I asked Dirk, "What was that all about? Did you know those people?"

"I can't talk about it right now. Later. That was just something I had to do. We've got other things to attend to."

We walked on quietly for some time before he asked, "Did you know that I have three cell phones?"

I told him that I didn't.

"Yeah. I've got my regular one and two for spare uses. They help me to liven things up."

"What are the other two for?" I asked him.

"Well, one's the CHUB number. That's the one you called. I leave it off most of the time. The other one's for miscellaneous use. I used it when I was pretending to be your attorney for the job interview."

"Did you actually seek out the CHUB number, or did you just luck out?"

"I lucked out. I got the two other phones with the intent of using them to keep things interesting. I worked out the possible spellings of the digits as they correspond to the keypad on the phone and I got CHUB. Hence..." he pulled off his bag and opened one of the front pockets to reveal some leaflets for his weight loss initiative along with some of my word pictures. "We're going to post some of these up around the streets."

"My word doodles too? Why?"

"Because they might make someone stop and consider something... anything at all."

I took some of the leaflets that Dirk offered me and watched him pull a roll of tape out from his bag. "So why bother with all of this, Dirk?" I asked him, suddenly seeing the idea as more ludicrous than I had originally thought it to be.

He pulled a strip of tape loose and bit it off. "Here, give me one of those." I handed him a leaflet and he walked over to a streetlamp and began to fasten it on. "I have a reason for the 'keeping it interesting' philosophy," he began, ripping off another strip and applying it to the side of the poster. "I feel that life is about two things: being kind to others and having a good time while you do it." Another strip removed, he finished up and motioned for me to walk on. "So, I like to do this kind of thing to amuse myself and hopefully get through to someone every now and then."

"This 'sort of thing'," I repeated, removing a new cigarette and struggling to light it with a hand full of leaflets, "seems... not very helpful." Successfully lit, my cigarette began to burn against the wind.

"What so you mean?" he asked, eyeing up a new pole and taking a new strip from his roll of tape.

"Well, it's just that... it seems like all of this, like the snorkel thing at the platform and the fliers and... it just seems that this stuff is more for you than for the goodness of... well, anything."

Dirk waved my wafting smoke away from his face. "Yeah. I suppose you're right. Here, can you get downwind from me or something?"

I obliged and moved off to the side, moving past an old man that glared at me and covered his face. I gave him a dirty look. "Fuck," I said. "This guy's walking a crowded busy street full of goddamn car exhaust and he's cowering from my cigarette. I'll never get that."

"People don't like smokers," Dirk said.

"I'm not fond of your implication."

"What, that smokers aren't people?"

I gave him the stink eye and blew my smoke out into the street, off to mingle with the car fumes and waves of steam flowing eerily from the sewers. "So why bother with this stuff?" I asked him. "What's the big idea?"

Dirk finished with the flier on his second pole and bade me walk some more. "You're right," he said. "This stuff is more for me than for anyone else. The chance that I'll actually affect someone is slim and it's an awful lot of effort for such a little payoff. But I take pride in it. It gives me something to do, makes me feel like I'm unique, you know?"

The taste of cigarette without coffee was starting to sour my mouth. I flicked the butt off into the street, aiming at a gutter and missing it entirely. "So what do you do to help people?" I asked.

"As if you need that question answered, roomie."

The sudden acid in his voice as he found a new pole made me weary. "Look, Dirk I didn't mean it that way. I know you're helping me out in a big way..."

"Then why ask the question?"

"I don't know. I guess I'm trying to pry more information out of you. About the associates, about that guy Phil back there, you know..."

"About my past?" Dirk asked, pushing hard on the final strip of tape on pole number three.

"Yeah," I said. "I'm curious. I want to know."

"In due time my friend. In due time."

Dirk and I put up the remainder of the fliers and headed back home on the train, the sun just starting to set on the rush of the city as we headed off into pseudo-suburbia to ignore all the dirty laundry we had piling up somewhere between us.

Fourteen

All Work and No Danger

"ALISTAIR AND SMYTHE, CHARTERED Accountants, how may we assist you today?"

This was how I answered the phone, but not how I greeted people entering the door of the small building where Dirk had conned me a job. When they entered the front door, I added a "Welcome to," and dropped the "how may we assist you". This was company protocol.

I was quickly learning the secretarial ropes in my new position. Not that there hadn't been a bit of faltering. Ron seemed afraid of me.

Ron, as it turns out, was Ronald Litke, Director of Human Resources. I found this hilarious. This was a small accounting firm with a staff of about twenty. The very title of Director of Anything was unnecessary. No one else seemed to even have a title so far as I could tell. Mr. Alistair and Mr. Smythe just went by Mr. Alistair and Mr. Smythe despite being presidents and partners of the company. I had yet to meet them in person. It appeared that the both of them preferred to work from home. They left the office in the care of one Gerald Forsythe. He too, it seemed, remained title-less.

Gerald took an instant dislike of me. I was loving the freedom the job afforded me. My tasks were to answer the phone and to file things. Every now and then, I had to be polite to a visitor while they waited for an appointment with one of the accountants, or bring Ron a coffee, but that was it. I was free to work at my own pace, no lunch rush, no line up, no attitude adjustment lectures. It helped that I was in a place where I respected that it was supposed to be a formal environment. I got that people did not want a clown or an apathetic, disillusioned, misanthrope handling their calls and filing their forms.

Every day, Dirk had a plan laid-out for me upon waking. I would find it on the kitchen table. He would write out what to eat, what chores to do and outline any miscellany that I was to take care of during the day. I hadn't seen him since my first day of work. The first five days on the job had been rough, but I was getting the hang of things quickly. I worked five days straight and followed Dirk's lists, doing the dishes, vacuuming the living room and seeing nothing whatsoever of Dirk. It felt good to be getting into a routine. After the first five days of work, I had two scheduled days off. It was strictly a Monday-to-Friday, nine-to-five affair at Alistair and Smythe, Chartered Accountants. Saturday, there was no list from Dirk, only a note:

Don't Do Anything.

It seemed that Dirk followed a traditional workweek as well.

I spent my days off scratching down a few pages of prose, smoking and puttering about. I ate and cleaned up after myself, doing the dishes after each meal, assuming that I better keep to the routine, not lose sight of the goal. I saw nothing of Dirk or the Associates for the entire first week. It wasn't until I came home on the Monday beginning my second week on the job that I first encountered Soup, lounging on the couch, doing a crossword puzzle.

"Hey," he said, urgently, and not in the friendly hello kind of way. "What's a twelve letter phrase for comeuppance?"

"What, you don't have an easier clue for me?"

"You're the writer," he said, challenging me.

"I don't do crossword puzzles," I said. "I prefer those other ones, the Sudoku things."

"I fucking *hate* Sudoku. Numbers bore me. Crossword's more of a challenge."

"You got the day off today?" I asked.

"Nah, just a half day. Only scheduled for four hours. Blessed shift, that. What about a five letter word for spear?"

"Spear?" I offered.

"Yeah, spear," he said.

"No, 'spear'," I tried again.

"What the hell are you talking about?"

"Spear's a five letter word for spear."

"You're an asshole, Cheesebomb."

"Lance."

"Your name isn't La... oh." Soup fit the word lance into his puzzle. "So now we're looking for a twelve letter phrase for comeuppance with the fourth letter from the end being an 'e'."

"I've got nothing," I said, sitting down on the sofa against my better judgement. "Where is everybody? I haven't seen anyone all week."

"Dirk wanted us to stay out of your hair. I think he wants you to get in the habit of being a self-sufficient individual."

"So why are you here now?"

"I like the couch," he said.

I got up from the sofa. "You want a drink?" I asked, making me way towards the kitchen.

"Yeah, sure, Coke."

I re-entered the room with two cans of cola and set one down on the table in front of him. I wasn't fond of Soup, or any of the Associates really, but I hadn't engaged anyone in a conversation recently and was begrudgingly lonely.

"What about a three letter slang word for 'like'?" he asked, and then, "Oh, 'dig'. Speaking of 'dig', how are you digging your new job? How's life as a secretary?"

"Not a fan of the heels," I said, not wanting to become indignant, but doing so anyway.

"Got your sights set on marrying some rich broker yet?"

"There aren't any 'brokers' at an accounting firm," I countered.

Soup reached over and cracked open his soda. "Whatever. Hey, mind if I smoke a joint?"

I shrugged. Soup reached next to the couch and opened a drawer on the end table. He reached inside and procured a small baggie of pre-rolled pot and a lighter. He took one of the little white darts out of the bag, resealed the zip-lock and stuffed it back in the drawer, closing it with a slam. Nothing here seemed entirely hospitable.

I desperately wanted to ask Soup about why Dirk had been homeless, about how they'd met. I knew Soup would have none of it, but since he'd mentioned it, the thought of what had happened to cause this motley crew to share one roof had occupied my mind on more than one occasion. Dirk would be the one to explain it, had almost explained it on the street while they were taking up those posters, but I was eager to learn and tired of waiting.

Soup lighted the joint and settled back in with his paper, scribbling in the answer to another clue.

"What did you get?" I asked him.

"Joust. A five letter word for 'competition on horseback'. Now we're looking at a twelve letter phrase for comeuppance that goes J-blank-blank-blank-D-blank-blank-blank-E-blank-blank-s."

"What was the 's'?"

"Sour," he said, exhaling a foul smell into the air.

"What do you do anyway?" I asked him.

"What do I do, what?" he asked.

"For a living, what do you do?"

"I work at a restaurant. Dishwasher."

"Do they call you Soup?" I asked.

"They call me what's on my nametag."

"And what is that?"

He took a long toke on the joint, more reeking marijuana stink. How I hated that smell. "What's on my nametag," he said, speaking weakly while holding the smoke in his lungs, "is my first name."

"Chicken Noodle?" I guessed.

He ignored me. "Four letter word for 'unattractive'. That'll be ugly," he said, writing in the letters as he spoke. "Now it starts with a 'ju'." He didn't say the letters, J-U, but rather pronounced them together.

"Why won't you tell me your name?" I asked.

"It's our system," said Soup.

"Your system?"

"We don't use real names in the house, just like we didn't use real names on the street."

"So Jimmy's name isn't Jimmy?"

Soup shook his head, blowing out smoke that crowded around him in a halo as he shook.

"And Rob isn't Rob?"

"Nope. And before you ask, *Cheesebomb*, Dirk isn't Dirk."

"I kind of assumed that," I said. "Whose real name is Danger?"

Soup shot me a look that said I didn't get it. "We just don't bother with that. We aren't close to one another, we aren't close to you, and there's no need for 'real' names in our relationships. We go by what we choose, and we don't choose our real names." He looked back down at the puzzle. "Five letter word for 'shy'?"

"Timid," I said bluntly. It was time for me to get on with my evening, make dinner and get to bed.

"Good, yeah, 'timid'," he said. "That leaves us with a phrase beginning with J-U-blank-T. What are you making for dinner?"

"Just desserts," I said.

"What, no meal plan from your old buddy Dirk?" he asked.

"It's the answer to your comeuppance clue," I said. "And as for your question, chicken. For one."

I left the room and took my soda back into the kitchen.

Over the next four days, I encountered not a soul in the House of Danger.

The following Saturday morning, after two weeks on the job, Dirk would finally reappear.

Fifteen

Lesson 5:
A Prelude to Pain

"THERE'S NO WAY IN HELL," I spat.

"It's important," Dirk protested, "that you try."

The setting was once again the kitchen table. It seemed that Mr. Danger tended to avoid the living room as often as I did. The permeating feel of discomfort in this house resonated most strongly from the communal living room and no doubt Dirk wanted as little to do with being uncomfortable in his own home as I did. That being said, it is uncomfortable enough for me to be an admitted failure of a human being who chose to live with a stranger for a month rather than manage life on my own. If a man's home is his castle, Dirk's had been penetrated from within, the Trojan horse was his own generosity and his discomfort was entirely his own.

Hate was on the brain this morning. I had awoken too early for a weekend, this being the second couple of days off afforded me in my new career and I had intended to enjoy them by sleeping in. I had planned to sleep until noon Saturday, eleven on Sunday and try to weasel my way back to seven AM on Monday. This was not to be. My internal alarm had reconfigured itself and my intent to stay in bed had been thwarted by an untimely alertness and a very full bladder. Up at eight, I puttered around the house, making breakfast for one. I hadn't seen Dirk in two weeks, and I had no reason to suspect that I might see him now, even though my time here was drawing to a close and we had only completed four of the seven scheduled life lessons that Dirk had planned. I was surprised when Dirk had appeared while I was munching and had inquired where I had put his breakfast.

Ever the ungrateful guest, I had patted my belly.

"It was delicious."

"Ha ha."

"So where have you been?" I asked, mouth full of bacon.

He shrugged. "Thought I'd let you fly solo for a while. I see you've been attending to my notes?"

I nodded. "House is clean, food has been digested and I've not yet missed a day of work."

"How is the job?" he asked, filling a cup with the thick black coffee I'd nearly mastered the brewing of.

I swallowed a lump of meat. "I'm getting the hang of things quickly. I think Ron's scared of me still."

Dirk laughed. "Speaking as your attorney, I think he's even more afraid of me." He took a seat at the table, dragging the legs of his chair slowly along the floor before sitting, the sound cutting into my head. I thought of fingernails, freshly cut, trying desperately to scratch an itch. I shuddered. "Someone walk on your grave?" he asked.

I shrugged and finished my eggs as we sat in silence.

Dirk was the one to break it.

"So we're doing another lesson today," Dirk said.

"I figured as much. I assumed that when you popped up next it would be time for whatever's on the agenda."

"I want you to visit your parents." Dirk looked at me with a deadly serious expression that I was not used to associating him with. Now we're into the angry bit. The NO WAY IN HELL bit. This is where he told me that it was important that I try. I said nothing. I wished my pate was full of food so I could throw it at him.

"I know, this isn't something that you want to do," he said, finally breaking the silence.

"Damn right I don't. I told you I wasn't fond of them."

His stern look altered slightly, becoming the face of a doctor who's got some bad news for you. "I know you said that they kind of shrugged you off, but…"

"Shrugged me off?" I asked incredulously. "Shrugged me… fuck, they flat out *ignored* me. It wasn't a shrug. It was considered and wilful avoidance. You'd have thought I was a leper."

"You didn't sound this upset when we talked about them in the restaurant when we first met."

"That's because I wasn't being asked to interact with them," I snarled. "I won't do it."

"I'm asking you to do it for me."

I laughed derisively. "That means absolutely nothing to me," I shot out at him, unthinking and uncaring. "I want them to come crawling back to me."

"They aren't going to," he said. "And I'm glad to see that all my help has been thankless."

I realized what I'd just said. "I'm sorry, I didn't mean it that way."

"What way did you mean it?"

"I meant it in the way that I will do anything to avoid meeting up with those two people. And besides, I can't even visit my Father. He's living in some other city. All I have is his phone number."

"Then give him a call."

"Why do you even care if I visit them? What is this going to do for me? Am I going to suddenly forgive all the sloppy parenting and neglect and go lovingly into their arms just because they produced me at some naïve stage in their lives? You know, I'm half-convinced my Mother got pregnant on purpose so she could divorce my Father and have a steady child-support-related income streaming her way regardless of her current state of employ. Gotta have that booze money." I took a final swig of my coffee, slamming the mug down on the counter.

"They're your parents whether you like it or not. They brought you into this world. Doesn't that mean at least something?" Dirk looked not at all as hurt as he forced his words to sound.

"That's a fucking cliché," I said. "A fucking weak cliché. A person owes their parents nothing."

It was Dirk's turn to sigh for a change. "You don't think giving you life is worth anything?"

I shrugged.

"It's not like you'll ever have to do it again if you don't want to."

A quiet glare was my reply.

"All I'm asking you is to do it for me as a favour," he tried again.

"What kind of favour is it to you? You've never met them. You know nothing about them. Fuck, you don't really know all that much about me. I was elated when I got to leave home. It was the happiest moment of my life. I don't want to do this." I paused for a moment while Dirk took an awkward sip of coffee. "You know," I went on, "not only do I not want to do this on principle, but the fact that I'm not... I'm not good at being a son..."

"You seem like you'd be a fine son to me," Dirk interrupted.

I sniggered. "All that proves is that you're a better parent than they'll ever be. You should have kids. I mean that. Go off and father some young."

Dirk placed his coffee down and folded his arms. "I took you in here to help you and you said you'd go along with all my whimsy."

"Are you trying to guilt me into it?"

We stared hard into one another's eyes.

"I'm not trying to guilt you into this," he said.

"That's what it sounds like to me," I replied, ironing out the sneer that kept trying to erupt on my face.

"Well, in all honesty, how do you think you could counteract that and make it sound like I'm being unreasonable?"

"What does that even mean? You try and guilt me and then ask me to prove how you can't possibly be guilting me?"

"Yeah, I am. What are you going to say?" Dirk took up a mocking tone, speaking as though the words were coming through some caricature of my mouth. "Oh, you may have taken me in without knowing me, fed me, got me a job, brought me just that little bit more out of my shell and got me writing again, and you expect me to do something I don't want to do? Well ho-ly shit."

Tears began to well up in the sides of my eyes.

Dirk looked at my mangled expression and stood up, affording me a little dignity, looking away as he took his cup to the coffee machine to refill. With his back still turned, he continued. "There's a reason I'm asking you to do this, you know. I'm not some fucking... sadist. I'm not trying to tear you up into little pieces. There's a real honest to goodness reason."

I swallowed hard, kept down the lump. "And what is that?" I asked with a paper voice.

"You'll find out tomorrow," he said. "I don't... that's not on the lesson plan for today."

Fuck you and your lesson plan, I thought.

"Think about it," he said, and with that, took his fresh coffee and left the room.

A tear rolled down my cheek.

I sat at the table trying not to think for as long as I could manage. Every time my Mother's face floated through my head I swatted the thought down hard. I was employing the Tennis Pro of my thoughts, pitting it against one of those damned machines that hurl ball after ball at you from across the court, training you, making you stronger. My Pro fared mightily at first, a ball bearing my Mother's face flew with a *shuck* from the machine and he gave it the old backhand, *swish* and sent her flying. My Father's face came next and this one hit with a smash and lobbed back across the net. My Pro was keeping time with his feet, bouncing from the ball of the left foot to the ball of the right, back and forth and *smash* went the balls, each one caroming off the ground and sailing away into the distance. It quickly became too much. My poor Tennis Pro was unprepared for such an infinite barrage. He began to lose steam, began to cramp up, began to lose his cool and started to hit the air, slicing it with a racket that was fast becoming worn from overuse. Soon enough the balls started to pelt him, firing faster and faster, and finally, with one resounding and sickening *smuck* — a single ball to the groin felled the poor Pro and reduced him to an extra in some bad comedy film, felled by a cliché prop device and earning him the cheapest laugh possible.

I was weeping openly now and it was because of the noise I was making, the pitiful racket, that I climbed from the chair and smuggled my coffee out to the front porch. The strangers could gawk as I pulled myself together. I would let them. It was only fair.

As soon as I had managed to stop weeping like a goddamned fool, I abandoned my coffee cup on the stoop, lit a fresh cigarette and struck out in the direction of my

Mother's home. Dirk wanted a fucking show, I'd give him a fucking show. I would visit my Mother and I would phone my Father and I could tell him all about it so he could file it away and feel smug like he'd somehow made a fucking difference.

Sixteen

The Fox and the Walrus

M Y MOTHER IS A fox.
This is not an Oedipal statement. I call her a fox not because of her looks, but because it is true, it is literal. I call her a fox because she walks on all fours and is covered in red hair. I call her a fox because she lives in a hole that is most often referred to as a foxhole. I call her a fox because she has rows of sharp teeth; because she is sly and manipulative. This is why I call her a fox.

When I go to visit her, I bring two chickens. She prefers live, the taste of the warm blood has a soothing effect. I cannot bring myself to do this. I take dead chickens and though they are not preferred, they will keep me from being berated more than usual. The chickens are a peace offering. Today, I can only find cooked ones, the store I normally go to for fresh on the spot and recently plucked meats is closed and I have to settle for barbeque style cooked whole chicken from the local grocery store. The smell is too much to take as they sway in their plastic bags dangling from my fist and I seriously consider eating them on the sidewalk, ripping strips of greasy meat from their upside-down carcasses and ignoring the fox in its hole.

I cannot do this.

Thank God the entrance to the burrow, her den, is big enough for me to get through. In the past, she had made sure that it was too small. Perhaps she had been waiting for my visit. It had been a while since I last tried and upon arriving and finding that I couldn't squeeze myself through the earthen hole, I turned back, not wanting to dig and knowing that she did not want me to dig. I had eaten those chickens, and I now grinned as imaginary slicks of chicken fat slid down my chin.

I descend into the hole, and though it gets smaller as I make my way through, I am able to squeeze myself and my parcel into the entrance to the den proper. There is a wooden door with a brass knocker. I ignore the knocker and use my fist, preparing for the direct conflict this visit will entail.

There is a pause. There is a long pause. There is a scuffling sound, a dragging sound and then a sniffling at the bottom of the door, and I can almost see her pressing her snout to the jamb and savouring the smell of my gifts.

The door creaks open.

"Son!" she exclaims, tongue moving across her teeth, eyeing not me, but the plastic bag filled with pre-seasoned meat.

"Left the skin on for you," I said, dropping the bag in front of her and pushing my way past into the den. "I know how you like it."

"I prefer them breathing," she said, nuzzling the bag open with her snout, "But this will do."

I sit myself down on the floor and take it all in. The room is sparse. There is barely any light and all I can make out is the frame of a sofa shaped object and a dim television glow from off in the other room. Mother dragged the bag into the center of the dirt covered floor, just in front of me and relieved the chickens of their meat as she began to speak.

"What brings you here?"

"I haven't seen you in a while," I said. "Thought I'd drop by and see how things were going." I could barely make her out in the gloom.

She tossed back her head and let a thick slab of meat fill her throat. "Oh, things are OK. Are you working?"

I shrugged. "Seems that way. You?"

"I'm still looking," she said. "It's hard to find a job when... well you know." She gestured around the room with her nose in the air making an arc.

I nodded.

"School?" she asked. "Girlfriend?"

"No and no. Not interested in school and never have been very good with women. Working on it though. You know that. Always looking."

"I've met someone," she said, pausing from her feast to stare at me and lick her paws a little, delicious pawed over chicken dribbles being whisked away by a long canine tongue.

"Oh," I said. This conversation was fast becoming what I had hoped it would not. She had a way of making things sour quickly.

"And I'm in school," she added. "He's paying for it."

I sighed. "What are you taking?"

"Oh, this and that. Psychology mostly. I bet I could psychoanalyse you."

"Who's the guy?"

"He's not 'the guy'. He's Willard."

I laughed. "Willard? Where did you find him? Victorian England?"

"He's a good man," she said. "A wasp. Works in waste management."

This was Mother's way of saying that he too was unemployed. If there was one vice my Mother is trapped with, it is television. Nobody works in waste management. Except maybe Tony Soprano. Oh, how she loved her gangsters.

Mother scurried through the room, with a bone in her mouth and leaped into the small hovel where the soft glow of the television had been emanating from. I uncurled myself from the floor and followed her into the next room, stooped to keep my head from slamming against the ceiling which I always thought would collapse one of these days.

"You never call anymore," she said.

"Phone doesn't work. Don't have one, I mean."

"You don't have a phone? Can't you pay the bills? Look, if you've come for money…"

"Stop," I said, "Just stop. I can see you don't have any."

"And what is that supposed to mean?"

Judge Judy nattered in the background about some lowlife landlord.

"Look can we turn this thing off?" I said, moving to do just that when she stopped me with a bark.

"I'll just turn it down," she said. "I like the light."

She mashed her paw down on the remote in a practiced way that brought the volume down to a whisper. She did not mute it. There was a crack from her jaw as the bone she'd brought in split in her mouth. "Don't stare," she muttered, eyeing my visible disgust as the crunching on the bone fragment continued. "It helps my teeth. Or so I'm told."

"I must've missed that *Cosmo*," I said.

"So why is it that you don't have a phone? Or was that just a line?"

I sighed, settling back down on the floor in front of her.

"I don't have a phone because I'm between houses."

"Between houses?"

"Yeah. I'm staying with a friend while I sort a few things out."

"What friend."

"A friend. You don't know him."

"Not... a her?"

"No, a him. No, I'm not gay."

Mother closed her mouth. I had sensed that one a mile off.

I continued: "I recently had a bit of a crisis and I met someone who's giving me a hand."

"Why didn't you turn to me?" she asked.

I had to stifle a laugh. A moment ago she didn't have a penny for me and suddenly she was stunned that I didn't turn to her for help and guidance in a time of crisis.

"Well? Why didn't you turn to me for help? Some stranger is better than your Mother?"

"Just because you don't know him doesn't make him a stranger," I said. The bone grating in her teeth was starting to madden me.

"I think I know what's best for my son. You know, it hurts me when you do this kind of thing."

"What kind of thing?"

She changed her voice, a soothing and practiced matronly lilt that she trotted out when she thought she was losing the crowd. "It hurts me to think you don't feel you can turn to me for help."

"Well," I said, "His place is decidedly less dank. It's not in the middle of nowhere, and I don't have to contend with this week's Foster Dad."

The bone in her mouth shattered with such force that I was afraid her teeth might've gone with it. "And just what is that supposed to mean?" she asked, the motherly tone long lost and vaporized along with the fragments of chicken carcass bleeding marrow in her mouth.

"You know what that means," I said. "For one, our conversations never go well. You don't seem to think you ever did anything wrong and you always turn things around on me."

"I don't turn things around on you," she said. "You're always the one turning things around. Whatever suits your needs. I need to be a monster for you to come to grips with yourself. This is just like I learned in class: you're jealous. That's what this is all about. You're upset because I'm with someone who takes up so much of my time that I don't have any time left for you. You're feeling left out." She chuckled to herself, at me, triumphantly and snidely.

"I'm not jealous of anything," I said, quelling the anger inside of me and knowing that just like my last visit, and the visit before that, I was going to leave here feeling like the bad guy, the guilty party; and she would be smug in the satisfaction that she still had me on the line. "I'm not jealous of a goddamn thing. What I am, is... You know what: no. I'm not going to do this. I'm not going to give in. I'm going. I'm just... going."

I stood up to leave and noticed that the paw she had started licking disinterestedly was covered in welts.

"What's wrong with your paw?" I asked. In the dim light of the TV I noticed more welts now, welts I hadn't noticed before, on her snout, her ears. There must have been more under her fur, deeper ones I couldn't make out. "What is wrong with... did he do this?"

"Did *who* do what?" she asked, tucking the paw under her slight frame, trying to hide it from me.

"Are you going to try and hide your face too?" I spat. "What are you doing? You've been through this before, and every fucking time you say you've 'had enough'. You preach on-and-on about how 'you're never going to let another man treat you like shit' and look how you end up!"

"Don't you swear in this house!" she yelped, growling and standing on the sofa, trying to puff herself up and look bigger than she was. "And don't pretend like you know what's going on."

"I don't have to fucking pretend," I said, ignoring her fierce growling at the second curse I uttered in her precious hole. "I can put two-and-two together. You are dating a wasp, you have a history with violent men and, OH!, lo-and-behold, here's some fucking stinger's welts on your damn face! How stupid do you think I am?"

"You know what, you get out of this house. You leave right this instant. I don't want you here anymore, ever again." She leaped from the couch growling and gnashing her teeth. "We're done here."

I raised my hands, slowly backing away from her angry teeth. "Fine," I said, "I'll go. I just want you to admit that he did this before leave."

"He's a wasp," she said. "It's in his nature."

I didn't say another word. I nodded, turned and opened the door, not once looking back as I closed it tightly behind me and made my way out of the burrow. There was no doubt that if I were to come back the next day, the hole would be built down again, too small for me to make my way through.

I fingered a scar on my shoulder as I headed into the open air. She had given it to me with those teeth of hers. I had told myself the same thing. She was a fox, it was in her nature. Maybe being numb to the pain you deal makes you numb to the pain you receive.

I'm not sure that makes it any better.

MY FATHER DOES NOT live in the same area of the world that I do. He lives very, very far away. I had always believed that this was to hide from my Mother. Perhaps to run away from alimony or something like that. Sometimes, I felt it was to get away from me. Maybe he just didn't like the responsibility. Maybe he didn't like to feel that he wasn't in control at every given moment. Maybe he just liked the cold.

My Father is a Walrus. I do not say this because he is fat. He is not. Well, actually, I'm not so sure about that. I haven't seen him in a very long time. I do know that his breathing is laboured, but I imagine that is more from smoking too many cigarettes than from layers of thick insulation weighing in on his lungs. He lives on an ice floe in the Arctic. It is hard for me to visit because I can never know precisely where he is. He moves as the current takes him. He spends all of his time fishing; has no television or telephone. Well, that's not entirely true. He does have a cell, just not a land line. It's hard to have a land line when you don't have any land. I imagine that not being able to have a land line was part of what attracted him to the open ocean. Another lost point of contact between him and my Mother and possibly, me as well.

I had a coffee in my hand and a cigarette in the other as I walked unsteadily up to the payphone, a roll of quarters in my pocket. Calls to an Arctic cell phone were never cheap. Setting my coffee carefully on top of the payphone, I reached into my pocket to pull out the coins and the small piece of folded paper with his number on it. After dialling, an automated voice told me to deposit five dollars to continue the call and caribou after caribou was fed to the slot on the machine.

I would start with a friendly hello.

"Hello!" I would say, mustering every ounce of cheer in me.

"Who is this?" would be his unsteady reply.

"It's me, your son!" the smile in my voice would seep through the receiver and bleed right into his ear, filling him with mixed emotions. In that instant he would go through his former life, how he met my Mother in a bar. The song on the jukebox would have been 'Witchy Woman' and he wouldn't have the foresight just yet to smile. He would flash to my birth, and then to the divorce and after this, would focus for what seemed like ages on all of the ensuing bitterness he suffered afterwards, all of the awkward half moments we shared together.

He would start small.

"So how's life?"

"Oh, it's all right," I would lie. These lies are best when two people don't speak to one another very often.

"Got a job?" he would say. This was a tactic to get around to what my Mother had asked me. About money. About me only calling because I needed it.

"Yeah," I would say, but would not admit to being a secretary. "I've got a job at an accounting firm. Tending the books."

At this point he would cough and I would be able to hear him light a cigarette, the metal swish of the lighter firing up and delivering a flame to the packed tobacco tip. He would inhale deeply. "So what're ya up to these days?"

"Oh, this and that," I would say. "I'm staying with some friends until I can get a new place."

"What happened to the old place?"

"Didn't suit me. Too big. Need something smaller."

"Oh yeah...

"Speak to your Mother lately?"

"Nah," I would lie. There was no point in bringing it up. Maybe he would take it as some kind of signal that I chose to call him and hadn't spoken to her. Even though I had. Even though I'd gone to her first. But he didn't know that. He might sense the lie though, or at least suspect a lie. That's why his response would be:

"Oh... that right?"

At this point, he would cough for what seemed like minutes, losing the phone between his flippers and I would hear it tumble and get wedged in the ice and snow. A bird might screech overhead and there would be creaks and groans as he shifted his massive self and cursed loudly, moving the snow aside with his paws to reach the phone. There would be a scraping sound as he wiped the slush from the receiver. This happened often during our phone calls.

"Sorry," he'd eventually say. "It's these damned flippers. Maybe I'll get me some of that plastic surgery. Get a few things corrected." This was supposed to be a joke. I would offer a sympathy chuckle.

"Heh-heh. Yeah."

"Do any fishing lately?" he'd ask. He was always asking about fishing. It was his only point of reference.

"Uh, no." I'd say, after a pause and sheepishly.

I would wonder if he knew anything about my interests. He didn't seem to have many. Or did he? How well did I know this creature, endlessly floating so far away from me. I'd only ever seen him in person a handful of times since the divorce. He'd never taken an active interest in seeing me, but then... had I taken enough of an interest? Was it even my place to do this? Should the son be the one making all the intimate gestures?

Suddenly I would appear upset for no reason.

"You gonna come for a visit soon?" I would say, bluntly and filled with force.

"Am I gonna what? Come for a visit?" I would sense the conversation turning on me. "You know what son... there's not a lot that's out there for me anymore."

Except me.

"I guess," I'd say, saddened suddenly, so quickly disarmed by feelings that I didn't have the slightest idea what to do with or how to deal with.

"Why don't you come out here?" he would offer. This was his usual offer when visits were discussed. Sometimes he would cite financial woes, sometimes it would be painful memories that kept him away and sometimes, there was just this apathy to the whole situation, just a general feeling of "I-don't-want-to-it-isn't-that-important-to-me". I would never press.

"Yeah, maybe." I would say, knowing how hard it would be to find him out there. Our call would become more distant now, and I would start to look for a reason to end the call. I would be able to hear the paper of the cigarette burning between his whiskers, smoke curling into the space between his tusks, lending a tobacco stink to his fish drizzled breath. I would just want to get off the phone.

"Yeah, you should come out here," he would say. "It's beautiful this time of year. The fishing's great. It can get a bit cold though. You'll have to get warm clothes ready." He would chuckle to himself a little. He left out that I would have to charter a plane to a small village where I would then have to charter a boat and would have to rely on cell phone service to triangulate where he was because he sure as hell wouldn't want to meet me in public.

"Tell you what..." I would begin, growing more anxious, more eager to end this call. "Why don't I look up some flights?" The lies would keep on coming. "I'll look up some flights, 'cause I've got a bit of money saved away and I could make it up there soon. Yeah, I'll do that right now. How about I do that and I call you back when I've got a plan?"

He would lie too. "That sounds great, son. You let me know. I'll make sure I'm available."

"Yeah, I'll do that right now. I'll call you back," I would say.

"Yeah, that sounds like a plan," he would say.

There would be a pause here before the good-bye. This is where I wanted the 'I miss you, Son' to be uttered. Just once was all I was hoping for. I just wanted to hear that one time. I'd say I missed him too, and that would be that. We wouldn't go as far as saying 'I love you' to one another. That wasn't something we did, wasn't something we would do. He wasn't that kind of guy. I wasn't that kind of guy. People like my Father didn't say 'I love you' to their sons. People like me wouldn't know what to do with that kind of information.

"We'll talk to you soon then," he would say, finally.

"Yeah," I would counter. "Soon."

The call would end and I would pretend that I was okay with that and I would light a new cigarette and get on with things, not looking up travel arrangements and not calling back, not now... not yet. The next time we spoke, he wouldn't mention it anyways.

The last coin had finally made its way down the slot. My call was being connected.

The operator spoke up: "The number you are dialling is too far offshore to be connected. Please try again later."

I hung up the phone on the receiver and watched as the coin return proved me a winner, pouring all of those quarters out through the slot onwards onto the pavement.

Seventeen

Bringing it to Boil

"So how did it go?"

I shrugged at Dirk's question.

After having been unable to call my Father, a feeling of rage had overtaken me. With my breathing rapidly accelerating, I stared down at the payphone receiver in my hand and with rapid, vicious thrashes I slammed the thing against the phone again and again until it broke, leaving the earpiece dangling from a few exposed wires. Somehow, that wasn't enough and the directory tethered beneath the phone became my next target. Try and I might, with uncoordinated and silly jabs and kicks, the thick tether held and would not break, the phone book swinging madly but not breaking free. Frustrated, my foot met with the plexi-glass side of the booth, hurting me and doing nothing to the see-through wall.

Still fuming, more frustrated than ever, I left, stalking off towards coffee, because surely coffee was all that could settle me now.

The nearest coffee place was next to liquor store where a man dressed entirely in denim did not seem to think that my brisk, stomping pace nor the scowl on my face should prevent him from accosting me for change.

"Excuse me, Sir?" said denim.

"What?" I asked with venom, eager for a chance to fight with some stranger.

"Sir, I'm from Invermeer and I came down here for a job interview. Unfortunately, I only had enough money for a one way ticket and am relying on the kindness of strangers to help me buy a ticket back home. If you could find the kindness to help me out it would be greatly appreciated."

I stared at him blankly, angrily. I looked up at the 'Liquor' sign above his head and back down to him while he waited for my response.

"You're trying to get home?"

He nodded. "Yes, Sir; back to Invermeer."

"And you're trying to save up money for a bus ticket?"

He nodded again.

"Greyhound?" I asked, barking the word.

"Yes sir."

"Then why," I asked, "Don't you go stand in front of the Greyhound station instead of the liquor store?"

The look on his face changed from pleading to stunned anger. "Are you calling me a liar?"

"Yeah," I said, "I guess I am."

I tried to stare him down, and spat on the ground near his feet.

His eyes shot into mine. "WELL, FUCK YOU!"

Whipping out my index finger, I waggled it accusatorily in front of his face. "Fuck me?" I asked, "Fuck *me*? FUCK YOU, YOU STUPID SON OF A BİTCH!" I moved in on him, causing him to back up a few steps and my balls grew bigger with each backward motion the man made. "You are a fucking liar and you know it. I can't believe you have the fucking gall to swear at me when you're begging for my goddamn money. I'm going to give you five seconds to apologize and then I'm going to lay into you like you've never fucking felt before. One…" My finger retracted into the fist my hand had become and I pulled back my arm like I was going to hit him. I was putting on a good show, making myself appear bigger than I was, playing at fearsome, electricity flowing through me. "Two…"

"Fine, man; geez. Look, fuck, I didn't mean it."

"I want a fucking apology," I said, "not an 'I didn't mean it'."

"I'm sorry. I'm fucking sorry, are you happy?"

"No," I said, moving forward another step, pushing him back another step, feeling my balls swell with testosterone. "I'll be happy when you book it the fuck out of here."

He muttered something under his breath and did in fact wander away. I was sure he'd be right back as soon as I was gone, but the anger made me feel so justified. I was right, goddamn it. The world was a hideous place and I was right to lash out at it. I was right to trash that phone booth and I was right to scare that beggar.

I bought my coffee, hit the train and sat sipping in silence on the ride home.

I had walked through the door feeling like a little shit when Dirk had asked me from the kitchen how things had gone. It was getting late and he had started on dinner.

"I vandalized public property and yelled at a bum," I said.

Dirk stopped stirring some pasta and looked at me blankly. "I see…" he said. "So it went well then? Did you go see them? When you just took off I figured you were going to at least try to visit your Moth…"

"Yes," I broke in, "I saw her. No, I didn't talk to Dad. I don't even know if the number I have for him is any good anymore. The voice told me the call couldn't be connected."

"Which voice?"

"The phone robot. The automaton that decides how much to charge you and whether or not to connect you."

"Ah."

"No, it didn't go well."

"What happened? With your Mother, I mean."

"She's a bitch," I said.

"But she's still your Mother."

I shook my fist at an imaginary something. "I don't care if she's my Mother or not. She's vile." I took a seat at the table, thudding down onto the hard wood.

Dirk tapped the wooden spoon he was stirring the pasta with against the side of the pot, draining off the excess water. "What did she say?" he asked. Setting the spoon down on the counter, he took a seat across from me.

"It basically amounted to the fact that Mother knows best and can help me through all of my trials and tribulations while cementing the fact that she can't take care of herself. She doesn't trust me to live on my own; and I don't trust her, period."

"Well, we've already decided that you aren't good at life, haven't we?"

"That's not the point," I spat. "I haven't seen her in how long, and the first chance she gets, she digs in at me. I'm not good enough for her and I never have been. She's going to school, supposedly, and I never have. She's got a boyfriend and I can't find romance no matter how hard I try..."

"But you don't try..."

"Oh, and I'm fairly certain that her boyfriend is abusive. I don't even begin to know how to handle that. It wouldn't be the first time either. I'm at the point where I'm sick of sticking up for her. It doesn't make any sense to me that she would make the same mistakes time and time again."

Dirk got back up to tend to the pasta, the water for which was now roiling over the top of the pot. "People fall into those traps over and over again. I couldn't begin to tell you why."

"It's because she's an idiot."

"It sounds like she needs your help," he said, blowing on the frothing pot to keep the water down.

I laughed. "I don't get any help from her and there's no way she's going to accept help from me, let alone admit that she needs it."

Dirk moved the pot of pasta to a back burner and shut off the stove. He sat back down and looked at me with about as earnest an expression you can get from a guy like Dirk. "Look," he said, "I'm sorry that it didn't go well, but like I said, there's a reason I asked you to do it. I feel like a bastard for asking you to. I know you didn't want to, but I think it was important that you tried."

I stared at his face for a moment, soaking in the expression on his face. It was the first moment of genuine emotion I'd seen in Dirk. He had let his guard drop. I briefly toyed with the idea of hitting him while his mask was off; tearing into him like I'd tore into that beggar.

But where would that get me?

"Why?" I asked instead.

" 'Why' what? Why did I ask you to go do this?"

I nodded.

Dirk sighed, still with profound earnestness of his face. "Tomorrow," he said.

I opened my mouth to demand an answer now, but he broke in again before I could speak.

"You okay with garlic sauce?"

I breathed deep, in and out, forcing myself to be calm.

"Yeah," I said. "Garlic is fine."

"Angel Hair Surprise."

"Do I get to know what this surprise is?" I asked indignantly.

"The surprise was the look on the angel's face when I took her hair. What did you vandalize?"

"The phone booth?"

"Did you kill it?"

"The booth?"

"The automaton."

"Are you kidding? That thing's unstoppable. After the apocalypse, all that will be left of our civilization will be Twinkies, cockroaches and the pre-recorded voice of the operator."

The sauce fell into the pasta with a sick *plop*, and the stirring sound leeched unpleasantly into my ears as I pretended for a moment that I wasn't still angry.

Eighteen

Lesson 6: The Dirge

"**H**ERE. PUT THIS ON."

I was doing the breakfast dishes. I turned to see that Dirk had laid a suit across the back of my breakfast chair. It was in one of those zipper covers, hanging loose over the back of the chair like a body bag filled with goopy remains.

"Where are we going?"

"You use too much soap."

"Huh?"

"In the dishes. You always use too much soap. Use less soap."

"Is that the lesson for today? Seriously, what's up? You don't quite seem yourself."

"I'm fine and would be more so if you used less soap."

"It's not like I can take any of it out. It's in the water now. And you certainly don't look fine. You look categorically mopey. You look sombre, like you're wearing a big sombre-ero. It's Mexican party time and you're the only one whose hat is frowning."

You're starting to talk like Dirk, I thought.

"Sometimes, Cheesebomb, you should feel out the conversation before you speak."

"What do you mean?"

"I mean, you should try to get a sense of what kind of dialogue you should be having with a person before you open your mouth."

This was the first I'd ever heard Dirk get defensive. This was new.

"If it's about the soap…" I hesitated.

"I'm feeling there's about to be an awkward pause here while you get what I'm trying to tell you. In this short pause, you'll suddenly realize that I'm not in a festive mood and that today's going to be Heavy." Somehow, Dirk was able to say the word with a capital letter. "Today is a hit man and he can swing a sack full of doorknobs like nobody's business. This is all starting to dawn on you in that small fraction-of-a-second pause that I'm sensing. You are pausing because you can see Today here in the room with us, loading up that sack of knobs ever so carefully. You can see Today picking out knobs like an old lady in the grocery store fumbling over the tomatoes. No, not that one, too dented, fractured… needs to be shiny and smooth. You can feel the weight of that sack before it even hits you over the head and then BAM!" He slammed a fist into an open palm. "With that, the silence is over, the pause has passed and you understand that today is a day filled with Pauses and Silence and getting hit over the head with a sack of doorknobs and that sometimes, less soap is more soap. Okay?"

Dirk left the room, leaving me visibly stunned in his wake. In the time that I'd known Dirk, he'd been bizarre, cheerful, quirky, thoughtful, and odd, but never argumentative and bitter. Whatever he had planned for today was not going to be a Good Time.

Because it was Saturday, I had the day off. After dealing with the phones and paperwork for a good three weeks now, I was starting to feel like I really had a handle on things. My job was becoming something I could actually do and which didn't involve a humiliating beanie and name tag. Dirk had not been around too often now. I figured he'd been giving me space to let me come into my own. He had become the Mother bird that was fed up with vomiting into her kid's mouth and had shoved him from the nest. Dirk was giving me the opportunity to fly or fall; sink or swim.

The associates were out doing their thing in the park, so the house was left to the two of us. Dirk had holed up in his room for the time being, so I grabbed the suit he'd laid out for me and went into my room to change. I unzipped the bag slowly, almost cautiously. The mood that my strange friend had left to linger made the suit feel ominous. The zipper fell away to reveal a headless figure, stone dead, the body having already rotted away. I half-expected the ashes of another man to slide out of the sleeves as I lifted the jacket by the coat hanger; its hook of a head. The momentary thought that the body of the man in the suit had been the most inept pirate imaginable gave me a quick smile. Captain McHoodhead finally laid to rest.

I changed into the pants, feeling the cold and perfectly creased wool slide over my skin like a cocoon in reverse, entombing me. Shirtless, I stood before the full length mirror that hung on the door. My pale belly bulged out a bit over the pants. They were a little too tight.

I ratcheted through my clothes for a white button up shirt and found the one I'd worn to work a few days ago only to discover a coffee stain I hadn't previously noticed. I'd never learned how to use bleach (or do laundry to any effective capacity), so the stain was now a part of the shirt. Maybe I'd learn to like it. It would be for my bohemian days.

I pulled on the jacket over the shirt, which fit just as snugly as the pants and buttoned up the front, covering my stain and restricting my breathing all in one go. I dug around my clothes pile for a tie and found a good solid black one.

My reflection was that of an awkward young man. I looked like a shitty salesman. Tucking the tie under the jacket I went outside for a cigarette before Dirk emerged to take us on our little trip.

My cigarette and I had a conversation about life.

"Hey!"

"What?"

"Don't light me on fire! What are you doing?"

"It's your purpose."

"It bloody well is not. Who do you think I am?"

"You're a cigarette. You're meant to burn."

"What? Me specifically?"

"No, not just you. All of you. Every cigarette is built to burn."

"Well... I'm not sure I agree with that. What are you meant for?"

"I'm not sure really."

"Maybe you were built to make my life a living hell."

"Actually, that's what you were built for. To make my life a living hell."

"But you just said..."

"Alright, I should have explained myself better. You were built so that you *could* be burnt. Your function, however, is to make my life a living hell."

"I don't know about that. I'm the one who's dying here."

"You're not dying. You're becoming something else. You're burning up, but your body is becoming ashes that will mix in with the earth and your essence is wafting away, up into the air. Can you imagine the view it must be having, so high up there?! I bet your essence can see for miles, high up over the trees, carried along by the winds, rushing at such tremendous speeds! You are experiencing the things of dreams up there, and yet you're down here worrying about a small fire. Don't be worried. You're even better than you were before. I, however, am getting cancer thanks to you. I am sacrificing you to sacrifice myself. So you see, I should be the one who's mad at you, not the other way around."

"Oh. Well, it still seems unfair to me."

"That's the way she goes my friend. That's the way she goes. Oh, hey, your times almost up. Good luck out there, eh? Thanks for all the trouble…"

I butted out and climbed back inside the house.

Dirk had come out of his room now. He was wearing a suit that fit far better than mine.

"Ready?"

"As ready as I'll ever be."

"That's the spirit," he mumbled. "Let's go. We're driving today. Which means you're driving today. Go get your keys. I'll meet you outside."

He turned and went, slamming the door behind him.

WE WERE ON THE freeway going on over to the other side of town. As usual Dirk wouldn't tell me where we were going, he merely gave me directions every now and then. The grim expression on his face gave me a hint. Today, I was going to learn who Dirk Danger really was.

"Turn left here, then your second right and we're there."

We pulled off of the freeway into a small suburban area. The row housing gave way to a huge grassy expanse dotted with stone monoliths and placards. He was taking me to the cemetery.

"Park anywhere," he said. "Just follow me when we've stopped. I'll take you to where we're going."

I stopped the car and Dirk removed himself from the vehicle, not pausing to wait for me at all.

There were no other cars in the parking lot. There were no other souls in sight. Dirk was easy to spot wending his way along a cobblestone path and then moving off into the field, passing between two rows of monstrous headstones. Finally, he came to a stop and turned to face me before I could get close enough to read the epitaph on the stone that he stood next to.

"Cheesebomb," he said after a moment's silence. "I'd like you to meet my brother. Derrick, this here's Cheesebomb. He's come to pay his respects."

I said nothing. Dirk filled the void.

"My brother here… he had some troubles. Have a seat, man… this'll be a while."

Dirk sat before me and I slowly followed suit. He tucked his legs akimbo, his fingers and their nails shredding the grass that lay before him. "Me and him," Dirk said, pointing over his shoulder with his thumb at the gravestone that sat stoically behind him, "we were thick as thieves. There was a bit of an age gap between us. He was two years older, but we shared the same sense of humour and we both had a penchant for pranks. The neighbourhood hated us. I remember this one house on our block was one of those gnome houses, you know the ones, with the stupid ceramic trolls littering their yard?" Dirk's face lit up for a moment as he began to reminisce. I nodded. I'd had a house like that on my block too. "Yeah, well, Derrick and I thought that they were stupid, so we used to go out in the middle of the night and move the gnomes over to this other house down the block. It was great, 'cause the gnome guy never suspected us for a moment, he just kept yelling at the poor sap whose lawn Derrick and I were sabotaging. The gnome guy kept getting madder and madder, 'cause he thought that this guy was stealing his gnomes. Derrick and I would hide close by and listen to their arguments. The gnome guy was really little, like, five feet tall, and the other guy was this fat dude who has kind of one of those New York-ish accents, so it was great fun. This little guy would run up and start angrily banging on the big guy's door and he'd yell things like, "I know you're in there, funny guy," and "Oh, this takes the cake, this *really* takes the cake!" All of his yelling came out in this tiny little voice with all of these words that sounded like swears from the nineteen-twenties. We half expected him to yell 'EGAD!' when he woke up in the morning to discover that his precious gnomes were missing. We couldn't have picked a better guy's lawn to throw the gnomes on cause this lawn guy was the polar opposite of the gnome guy. He'd answer his door swearing like crazy. 'I didn't fuckin' touch your dolls!' It was great! Calling them 'dolls' just made the gnome guy even madder and he'd start shaking and sputtering. The lawn guy was like, 'What the fuck makes you think that I'd take your goddamn dolls and put them on my lawn? Huh? Why would I steal something from you and put it out in plain sight? It's probably just some fucking kids. Go get your dolls and go home.' The big guy would slam his door and the gnome guy would yell something like, 'Shame on you, Sir! For shame!' and bustle about angrily collecting his gnomes. It happened like this every time until one time the gnome guy tried to hit the big guy and we could no longer hold in the laughter. The two neighbours quickly realized that the bushes were giggling and chased us out of there. We stopped doing it after that." Dirk's smile began to fade as he slowly shook his head.

I had no words, nothing felt right. I simply waited for Dirk to settle, to continue, to drink in what he had to and say what needed to be said.

He continued:

"Derrick died when I was young. Well, young-ish. I mean, I'm still young. I was nineteen and he was twenty-one." Dirk paused and looked over at the tombstone. "I've caught up to ya and then some, haven't I buddy?" There was no smile, no hint of mirth in the words that seemed like a forced joke, the kind that policemen must make when looking at a murder scene to make it more palatable. For a brief moment, to distract myself perhaps, I thought of David Caruso, hands on his hips, sunglasses on and head cocked offering some witty *bon mot* to the camera as he does at the opening of every episode of *CSI: MIAMI*.

Dirk feigned a chuckle. "He committed suicide, my brother."

I had to say something.

"That's awful," I tried.

"It's selfish," Dirk replied, still looking at the grave marker, his face slowly registering a scowl. "I still have his damn note. He actually left a fucking note. Why do they leave notes?" he asked me.

I hoped it was rhetorical.

"Seriously, I don't fucking understand the suicide note. It's enough to just do it; we fucking get it, OK!? We don't need to know why, we don't need to try to understand. It's the same shit, every time. Life's hard, things are unfair, my fucking girlfriend was in bed with another guy, another girl, what-the-fuck-ever." Dirk picked a blade of grass from the tombstone, carefully, making sure the white of the root came out with it. He placed the white of the grass in his teeth and bit down, severing the green and tossing it aside. "He said he was sorry. I'm sure that's a common one. It was school. He doesn't say it in the note, but it was school. He always thought that my parents, our parents, expected too much of him. They wanted him to be a doctor and seriously thought he would do it. My Father enrolled him, took him to the University, always pushed those grades and paid for the whole thing. It was that. I know it. They *pushed* him. I know it because they *never* pushed me. My grade would be poor no matter what they did. I was a slacker and an underachiever and it was all on purpose because I was better than all that. That's what I thought. I was above it all. I was so far above the teachers they could have been wearing stilts and I would have devoured them whole like some goddamned T-rex. Would've got them on the toilet too, like in *Jurassic Park*. Ultimate indignity, that."

I was so eager to ask him how it had happened. Was it razors? Was it a bed sheet noose in the closet? Overdose on pills, or drugs? How else did people do it? Not a gun. I didn't think people in Canada killed themselves with guns. I kept wanting to ask, the curiosity overwhelming me, and I knew he would never say, and I knew I could never ask. I kept distracting myself, keeping my breathing regulated, wanting a cigarette and damning decorum. Really wanted a cigarette.

"I can't help but feel like my parents pushed him because of me. They didn't want to end up with two slacker kids and maybe they already saw me as a lost cause. They wanted a better cut of that loin meat and they saw it in Derrick. I think it all mounted up, piled too high. He kind of mentioned it to me once. I'd just taken a trip to Mexico with some friends and I phoned him to tell him all about it. He sounded changed and distant and worried. He'd told me that 'things were going… well'. He paused like that too. I kept probing him about University life. He was living in a dorm at the U. The local University wasn't good enough according to my Father so he had been shipped off elsewhere. That was the worst of it I think. Anyway, I kept hounding him about how many times he'd been laid and how many beer bongs he's downed successfully and how many drugs he'd tried."

Another blade of grass pulled out firmly between his thumb and index finger was removed of its milk white root and cast aside. "Derrick got so frustrated with me. Kept telling me it wasn't like that. That was a movie. This was hard work and plenty of it. He didn't have time for things like that. Not if he wanted to become a fucking doctor. Two weeks after that he was dead. I was the last one in the family to speak with him."

It was time for me to speak again. I could feel it. "How did your parents take it?" I asked awkwardly.

"They died!" he spat and laughed, a real laugh this time.

I wasn't sure if he was kidding or not. Thank God he spoke before I botched it with my fat tongue.

"On the way to the funeral, they died. Car accident. Bad one. I had barely spoken to them that week. It takes about a week, did you know that? Your brother dies and they can't get around to a service until a week has passed. Do you know how many people have to be dealt with? The police, the school, the funeral home people, the people that make the tombstone, so many goddamned people. It's insufferable that you should be forced to deal with that many people at that kind of a time. It's worse still when your parents are too grief stricken to take care of much of it at all and you have to do the bulk of it on your own with a blank cheque or two from your rich daddy and eyes that just want to drown every person you meet with tears. Seriously, I envisioned that. The funeral home guy, that was the guy I had to deal with the most. We were in this room and he was having me choose a casket out of a fucking catalogue, like it's some IKEA brand accessory for today's dead person on the go. I picked the ugliest one. It was white and had these hideous flowers carved into the wood and it was inlaid with some cheap crushed velvet looking crap the colour of a bad '80s Mohawk. I pointed at the one and choked it on back, this welling in my throat and

I wished I could just let loose and kill him with my tears. I'd pick an ugly coffin for him too."

Dirk was getting angrier as he went along, and visibly trying to calm himself, stop himself from shaking. "I didn't go to either funeral," he said. I didn't show up. I don't even know what I did. It's like the whole thing was gone from my memory. I was supposed to be a pallbearer. I volunteered, foolishly thinking it was some grand gesture... for my brother, that is. Not for my parents."

"Are they here too?" I asked.

"Who? Mom and Dad? No, they aren't in the same cemetery. They are somewhere else, in accordance with their will. Why that place was good enough for them and not Derrick I can only guess. You know I've never visited them?"

"Never?"

"Not once," another blade chewed and tossed. "I told you I used to be homeless?"

"Yeah, you mentioned it."

"When my parents died, I hid from everything. They left money, a lot of it, to me and they left the house. Well, they left it all to Derrick actually, but I was second on the list. It wasn't the house I live in now. It was a bigger house, one for affluent types and I didn't want much to do with it. I sold it. Now, I'm nineteen years old, I've lost everything in the world to me and I had all of this money. You'd think I'd spend it all, mad with grief or some such bullshit. Make up an excuse to send myself on the bereavement world tour or something. But I didn't want it. I didn't want a cent of it."

"I can understand that," I said. I could. I wouldn't know how to react to that. It was blood money. His whole family went away and left thousands upon thousands of unsmiling green faces with no arms to hold him and no words to console him.

He nodded and his guillotine teeth demolished another carefully selected blade of grass.

"When I found out how wealthy I'd become by losing my family, I couldn't take it. All of that money just sat in my bank account. I spent some of it on hotels, until the house sold, because I just couldn't go back there. And then, after another month in a Super 8, watching TV day and night and living on room service, I decided I'd throw out everything but my wallet and some spare clothes and I rented a storage locker. Not a big one where you can keep everything, but the kind you get at a Greyhound station. Just a little locker. I put a padlock on it and stored the combination in my mind and I just went out and sat on the sidewalk for a very long time. Weeks. I kept a bit of money and used it to get some food here and there, but I didn't want the rest of that damned money. I didn't want to waste it in hotels and I... it just felt wrong. So I just started to live outside, on the cement. I slept there, I pissed in alleys and ate food with dirty hands from people who eyed me like I was going to take something. I was done, empty and alone on crowded sidewalks for a very long time. I'm not sure how long it was even. I didn't read the papers, started begging for coins. That's when I met the other guys. They were junkies mostly, not Soup, but the other two were. Actually, there had been five of us until an overdose. I started stealing. They helped me to start stealing. I was taught the best ways to steal. Soup showed me the finest method. We would go into a department store, do a quick run to the men's room, see if there was anyone in the stalls and if there was, we would reach over the top of the stall door. If we were lucky, some guy would have hung his coat there, or a bag from that hook just on the other side. Nobody in the middle of a shit gets very far after you take off with their stuff. Worked wonders. Kept me fed and gave me a bit of energy: the wrong kind of energy. The more and more I broke the law, the more I felt justified in what I had done. The worse things got, the more I was sure that I deserved it. We would hang out in the park all day, Robert and Jimmy getting stoned and Soup and me watching to make sure they didn't do anything stupid, just laughing and begging and stealing. I deserved it and I deserved worse."

"What changed?" I asked.

"What do you mean?"

"How is it that you came to where you are now?"

"The overdose was a part of it," he said. "There was another guy, Billy. He was the worst of us, into heroin. The other two didn't touch it, but he was heavy into the stuff and they liked him and worried about him. Your friends are all you've got when you're that far gone. They get it. They understand what's happening. They can commiserate like nobody else. That's why most people give up their old friends when they try to go straight. The old life is easy to fall back into. Billy died in an alley one night with us. We were all huddled into a bunch on boxes and Billy had too much and that was it. We didn't know he was dead until we woke up the next morning.

I didn't want to deal with it so I took off, left them there to deal with the body. Then I got caught stealing. I wound up in a holding cell for a few days, cause there's not much that the cops can do to a petty thief. I got a fine. And then... something just kind of snapped in me. I didn't know what the fuck I was doing. I'd been on the street for a year and there I was, running from another dead body and winding up even worse off than I already was. I didn't want to show up and see the guys again. I figured they'd be pissed. I bummed around for a few more days, trying to get my head straight. Finally I'd had enough and went back to my locker. I got out my wallet and my clothes and washed up in a sink, changed into something new, something that hadn't been stolen or found in the trash, put my own skin back on. Within a few weeks I bought a house. For a long time I didn't know what to do. I paced, didn't eat, didn't have a bed or any furniture. I couldn't stand being alone and I still felt like I was using my dead parents. I had to do something noble with the money."

"So you asked those guys to move in with you?"

"Yeah, sorta. They were pissed at first. Called me a liar, a poser. Like that song 'Common People'. I was 'slumming' they figured. Took them a while to come around, but they did. I'm still pretty sure they don't like me. I'm a charity giver being treated like a charity case. I don't know if they're clean, but they don't do drugs at the house. I barely talk to them."

We sat in silence for a very long time.

"Do you understand now, why I wanted you to try and visit your parents?"

"Yeah," I said. "I guess I do."

I looked over at the tombstone and noticed something that hadn't struck me at first.

"Dirk," I said. "Your last name really is Danger."

"Yeah," he said with a smirk he didn't quite mean, "But my first name's not really Dirk."

Nineteen

Lesson 7:
Shutter at the Thought

"So THIS IS IT, huh?" I asked Dirk, focusing the lens on the camera he'd provided for me until the cracked and peeling brown paint on the fence post came into focus.

"You're not off the hook yet," he said, looking up at the sky, blue and patchy with clouds like some surreal Dalmatian. "I've got two more surprises in store."

I knew well enough by now not to inquire about any surprises. I had just completed yet another week of work and had been so wrapped up in dealing with the visit to my Mother behind me, as well as absorbing our visit to the cemetery, that I hadn't realized that this was all coming to a close. I would no longer be staying with Dirk after tomorrow.

A dream had awakened me at five o'clock this morning. A nightmare. I can't be certain what it was about, but remember waking to the relief that I had simply been sleeping. I couldn't fall back into slumber, though I lay in bed for another hour with eyes shut and my head racing. I hadn't been planning. I had yet to receive my first paycheque. It was a week away yet, and I hadn't been planning. I didn't have enough money for a place. After tossing and turning for about as long as I could stand I got up, dressed without showering and rummaged through every drawer in the house before finding the phone book. I looked up every youth hostel in town, carefully wrote down their phone numbers and proceeded to call each one, pleased to find that all of them were fully operational in the wee hours of the morning. After three or four of them I stopped calling. On average, the price of the hostels was around twenty bucks a night. With what I had left, I could afford three nights and no cigarettes. With a cup of coffee in one shaking hand and a cigarette in the other I weighed my options on the porch. Had this been a stupid idea? Had it been worth it? Was I any better off now than when I met this madman named Danger?

Pro: I had a job.

Con: I had no home.

Pro: I felt a little better about my writing.

Con: I had no money.

Pro: I had come to terms with the fact that life will not bend to my will.

Con: I certainly couldn't ask my Mother for help.

Pro: I have become less defeatist.

Con: I have become more realistic.

Two cigarettes went down smooth. The third brought out a helping of phlegm. The fourth made me a little nauseous. The fifth went down smooth. A whole pot of coffee did nothing to slow the jitters.

The associates piled out of the front door at around nine o'clock. They said very little to me and I very little to them. Pleasantries were exchanged so thin and taut that they were liable to snap given any provocation. I would not be sad to see the last of them. I will never understand what these four men went through together, or what bizarre sense of honour made them feel that they should live under the same roof when they barely tolerated the situation at all, but I would not be sad to see them go.

When my ruminating brain ceased to function and decided that it required more coffee, I went back inside and found Dirk at the table, a new pot of coffee already made and two cameras on the kitchen counter.

"I've become a fan of digital," he said, watching me eye the cameras. "I used to think that 35mm was the only way to go, but the sheer *convenience...*"

"What's this?"

"This is the grand finale," he said, getting up to refresh his own cup of joe. "This is lesson seven. We're going to relax."

Hysterical laughter burbled out of my throat.

"What?" he asked, bringing the pot over to the hand I held out, mug extended, jittering.

"You wouldn't believe the morning I've had." I took the newly filled, quavering mug and transmogrified from a swaggering statue of nerves into a pile of laundry in a chair at the table.

"Oh, I'd believe it," he said, sipping loudly. "Oh, that's a little hot."

I downed the cup, heat be damned.

"I guess it's not quite hot enough."

"I've realized that..."

"No," he cut me off. "It can wait. We don't care about that yet."

"You don't even know what it is we're not caring about yet!" I hadn't meant to sound frustrated, but it came across that way.

"I know well enough that I don't need to know until tonight. We've got a nice big event planned and I don't want to spoil our relaxation time before the day is through. Only one more sleep until freedom, eh?"

I laughed again, a little more of my nerve spilling out of my throat, making the laugh sound forced and distant, an echo recreation of mirth belched up from the cavernous depths of my tar encrusted wind pipes.

We ate, finished the coffee and left the house, armed with our cameras.

Dirk and I now stood in front of a dilapidated fence in one of the alleys near the house. We hadn't walked far, but this didn't seem to be the point.

"You know," I said, sizing up another peeling and gnarled piece of fence for a photo, "it's always the uglier things that I find most beautiful."

"You once told me you didn't like pugs. That makes you a liar." Dirk gazed up into the clouds as he spoke watching their slow migration.

"Not that kind of ugly," I said, pointing to the fence. "This kind of ugly. I like my ugly to be weather-beaten fences, carelessly discarded tires, peeling paint and graffiti. That kind of ugly."

"I know more than one graffiti artist who would take offence to that," he said.

"Graffiti doesn't have to be ugly. There's an awful lot of it that's really not that bad, but that stupid shit," I said, "the 'tagging', that kind of crap. I lived in a place once when I was a kid where some idiot had plastered every building, newspaper box and telephone pole in a three block radius with his stupid tag."

"What was the tag?"

"It was the word 'virus' written in some bizarro cursive. That kind of thing, I have no place for. However, I do like to take pictures of that kind of thing."

"Cheesebomb, you are a man of great paradoxes."

I shrugged and snapped off a few rounds at my hideous fence and we kept on down the greenbelt. As we neared the park on one of the side streets in the neighbourhood, we stopped into a coffee shop for a couple of brews. Sipping our coffee, we headed down a steep hill and into the public park, empty of all human life, and rich in nature, armed with our cameras to capture it all.

"How come you aren't taking any pictures?" I asked Dirk. He had only taken a couple since we'd left the house, while I was on photo number fifty-one and despite my mood earlier this morning, was enjoying myself immensely.

"I haven't seen anything yet that I really wanted to get," he said and loudly slurped at the hot liquid bouncing in his paper cup as we lumbered down the hill.

"There's tons out here to get. You didn't like that fence?" I asked.

"Fence was okay," he said.

"What about the fire hydrant?"

"Didn't really grab me."

"Brambles?"

"Nah,"

"What about that hamshackle old gate?"

"Did you just say 'hamshackle'?"

"No, I said 'ramshackle'."

"No, you said 'ham-shackle'."

"I don't think so."

"You did."

"Well, I didn't mean to."

"I don't believe you."

"What is a 'ham-shackle', anyway, I wonder?"

"Something to keep your pig from running away, I suppose."

"A 'ramshackle' isn't something to keep your ram from running away though."

"Huh. Well isn't that a bit of a conundrum?"

We stopped at the bottom of the hill and Dirk dropped to the ground, crossed his legs and placed his camera on his lap. I remained standing and took out a cigarette, lighted it and breathed in a heady whirl of smoke.

Dirk looked up at me, then past me and back up into the sky, now slightly obscured by the thick leaves that canopied over us in the late afternoon sun. "I didn't really feel like taking pictures today," he said. "I just really wanted you to."

"Why?" I asked him.

He looked back from the clouds and at me once again. "When I first went to your apartment after we met and we loaded all your stuff up I was pretty amazed to see that you had no pictures whatsoever. You remember that?"

I nodded. "Yeah. I remember."

"Well, I thought you ought to have some. When we're done today, you keep the memory card and get these things printed. Hang a few of them up on your wall. Or don't. Whatever. I just... I just thought it would be nice is all."

"That is nice of you, but I don't know when I'm going to have a wall to hang anything on for a while." I paused for a moment, taking a deep drag of smoke and a sip of black coffee before continuing. "I was up early this morning, digging through the phone book. I think there's a decent hostel or two downtown that I can stay at until I've got a few more bucks together. I get my first paycheque next weekend and..."

"You've got a place," Dirk interrupted.

"Dirk, man. You've done enough for me," I said. "I appreciate the offer, but I can't stay with you anymore."

"I wasn't offering. I found you something."

"Found me something? Like a place?"

He nodded.

"Dirk I can't afford..."

In mid sentence a pair of keys hit me in the shin.

"Those are yours. It's a small place. Cheap and right near where you work. Third floor bachelor. Not a lot of room, but it's fine for what you need." He was looking up at the clouds again.

I picked up the keychain that had hit me in the shin. There were two keys dangling from a ring attached to a plain leather swatch with the Chevy logo on it. "Dirk, I can't accept this..." I said, trailing off. Of course, I *wanted* to accept it, but a combination of relief and the sense that I was being pitied were gnawing at me. It didn't feel right, but I wanted it to feel right.

"You have to. First month's paid. It's done and ready. You'll have two cheques coming to you next month. Don't blow them. Pay your damn rent and your bills. And don't say another word about it. It's done. You're out tomorrow. You'll have some pictures and a few stories and a job under your belt, and you'll be able to pretend like you're a real gen-u-ine adult."

"But..."

"Don't."

"Well..."

"Don't."

"I was going to thank you," I said.

"Oh. Well, don't. But you're welcome." Dirk put his coffee cup on the ground, steadied it on the slight incline until he felt it wouldn't fall over and lay on his back. He raised the camera up to his face and began to take pictures of the clouds as they rolled steadily on across the deep blue of the sky.

"I take it this was the first surprise?" I said.

"Yep," he said, still snapping the odd photo of the clouds rolling along. "We'll do the other one tonight. Sort of a send off."

I lay down near him, nestling my own coffee into the grass and tried my hand at a few of the clouds as well.

After a few minutes of silence punctuated by the sound of our digital snaps, Dirk spoke.

"You know," he said, "I don't feel close to you at all."

"Yeah," I replied. "I don't feel all that close to you either."

Twenty

A Sacrifice

"**H**ERE, TAKE THIS," DIRK said, handing me a box full of pornography. Full of *my* pornography. How I had amassed so much pornography I had no idea. Dirk's initial comment upon finding the stash in my home when we were moving me out was apt: I had an *assload* of pornography.

We had arrived home from our photographic excursion earlier in the afternoon. I decided to say nothing more about the keys to my new apartment. I had been surprised to discover that most of my things had already been moved there. It wouldn't have been much of a trip to cart the stuff over, and apparently Dirk had taken care of it when I had been out visiting my Mother. I hadn't noticed the stuff had been missing until he mentioned it. The only things that had yet to be moved were my clothes and the porno. The porno would not be coming with me.

"One more night," Dirk said, grabbing the leftover porn and motioning with his head for me to follow him. "Are you excited to be making a bee-line for freedom? Get out of this hell hole?"

"I've never understood why people say that," I said, hefting the ridiculous weight of thousands of naked woman and unread articles as we made our way to the back entrance of the house.

Dirk balanced the porno in his arm and opened the door to the backyard, which I had been surprised to realize, I hadn't ever set foot in. "What? 'Hell hole'?"

"No," I said, keeping the door open with my back as we pushed out onto the grass in our sock feet, "'bee-line'."

Dirk had a fire pit in the backyard, a small circle of bricks built up to contain the heat. He threw the magazines directly into the pit and motioned for me to do the same, pointing at the box and then into the pit with a grim face and an air of finality. "Why don't you like the 'bee-line'?"

"It doesn't make any sense." I threw my shame, box and all into the pit. "Have you ever seen a bee fly? They don't exactly make a straight line."

"Yeah, they don't seem like very efficient fliers."

"Then where did the phrase come from?"

"Maybe from an angry bee. They fly straight for the kill."

"Maybe that's why they call them 'bumble' bees, eh?" I jiggled my eyebrows up and down like an idiot. "Get it?"

"Your nomenclature is more suited to you than you could ever imagine, Cheesebomb. Wait here a moment, this is going to be huge."

Dirk ran off back to the house and left me alone with a tiny turret jutting out of the ground before me, filled with breasts of all shapes and sizes that I would no longer have the pleasure of wanking to. I was not unhappy to see it go. In fact, I was a little relieved, not least of all because the damn box was heavy. It was chocolate icing on the bitter-sweet cake of having lived here. Burned baggage.

When Dirk emerged, I was leafing through a magazine plucked from the beginnings of our bonfire. I looked up as he exited the house with the screen door slamming behind him. He had a very large bottle of lighter fluid.

"Just saying goodbye," I insisted and threw the book back into the pit.

"This is going to be sweet. Here," he said, passing me the bottle. "You do the honours."

"With gusto."

I stood over the pit, a woman staring back at me, pleading falsely with her eyes that she needed a man and fast, and emptied the entire contents of the bottle onto her face. I threw the bottle in as well. "You mind?"

"Mind burning plastic? Hell, I practically live for the stuff!"

"You know, I feel a little wrong about this."

"About what?"

"That woman's face was staring at me..."

"It's not like we're burning her," Dirk said.

"I know, but... it's a little weird..."

"We're burning a symbol of your old ways. You have to promise me after this that you aren't going to amass this kind of collection when you're back out in the real world."

I thought about that for a moment. "I'm not too sure..." I said. "I suppose I haven't really felt like looking at it or buying it at all since I've been here. I'm not sure if that was just the circumstances of... this... or... hmmm. I just don't feel like it. I'm not promising though. Well, not a collection like this anyway. If I buy one I'll at least throw it out when I'm through with it."

"That's good enough I suppose," he said. Reaching into his pocket he pulled out a small box of matches. "Here." He tossed them to me.

Naturally, I failed to catch them. Leaning down to pick them up, I became stuck again on the eyes of the model, staring out at me, hungry. I stood straight and took out a match.

"You know, I can't even go to the bathroom if there's a pair of eyes staring up at me from a magazine," I said.

"You're kidding me," Dirk laughed. "You think George Clooney on the cover of Entertainment Weekly can see you through his eyes on a magazine?"

"No... but... I have a bit of an issue with it... no pun intended."

"Just throw the match, weirdo."

I struck it, looked away and dropped the match into the pit and backed off immediately. The flames licked high and fast, quickly devouring the fluid and moving on to the pages upon pages of porno. The thousands of pages. God what a wreck of a life I'd been living. I briefly thought of the scene in Monty Python's *Meaning of Life* where Michael Palin starts singing about how every sperm is sacred. I smiled, thinking of the song, watching the whole thing razed in the pit.

I looked over at Dirk, who did not smile but stared trance-like into the flicker and spit.

"Dirk?" I asked.

"Yeah," he said, eyes unmoving, focused of the fire.

"Thanks," I said. "Thanks for everything."

"Yeah," he said, lost forever to the flames, "thanks yourself."

Tomorrow I'd be gone.

The glow kept on as the sky dimmed and we both sat in silence, warming our hands over so much spent flesh.

Twenty-One

Falling Up

"**D**O YOU HAVE ANYTHING that would be considered 'indestructible'?"

The fish store was a dangerous place for a guy like me. The clerk in his baby blue uniform led me past rows and rows of tanks, thousands of uneasy fish following our movements with worried eyes. A school of tetras bolted inside of a castle, fortifying against attack. A puffer fish hyperventilated; ballooning and deflating out of control. A little goldfish nipped at a hermit crab, perhaps determined to get it out of its shell, the only hiding place in sight, hoping that a naked crab would be a better catch. They knew that I was bad news.

"Indestructible?" the clerk asked. "Well, you might try a fighting fish. They are pretty solid little guys."

Laughter filtered through my teeth and echoed in the dank, moist air.

"You'd think so, wouldn't you?" I asked rhetorically.

It was time to buy another fish.

My life had been Dirk free for two weeks now, and things had been difficult at first. The apartment was indeed small, the bedroom and living room were one and the same, and there was a small kitchenette off to the side. The bathroom was separated and there was a tiny closet and that was it. Dirk had piled all of my things in to the center of the room and when I first turned the key and entered my new home, the sight of a lone pile of miscellany in an otherwise empty room filled me with despair. The sight of the four white walls with nothing but a small kitchen, a pile of boxes and a couple of doors made me think of the story that Jimmy had wanted to write. Someone had put me here as punishment and it was my job to find a way out.

Leaving the apartment was the only time I felt free. Work was still going well, and I had a paycheque under my belt after the end of my first week in my new dwelling. Work was the only thing that seemed to be going well however, as I was not eating and trying not to be in my empty room. I hadn't done any grocery shopping since moving out and had maintained a steady diet of coffee and cigarettes. Sleeping was done on a pile of laundry and garbage was placed in a loose plastic bag on the floor. Old habits are hard to kick.

After work, for a few nights in a row, I went to Dave's to see if I might spot Dirk. Maybe I'd find him and let him know that perhaps I'd left too early. Maybe I just wasn't ready yet and could still use a bit of a hand getting things together. Maybe I'd cry and tell him how bad things were. Night after night, Dave's played host to a cadre of colourful characters as I sat sipping an Orwellian Victory Gin and wishing that the establishment had not banned smoking inside.

On a particularly dour evening, the gin was taking its toll and thoughts of self-flagellation kept rifling through my head. Back to Mother's. It was the only way. That's what would have to happen. I would go back, admit that I had been wrong and that I still needed the help of my loving mother and we'd be happy together until we tore each other's throats out with teaspoons.

As I was imagining the sheer joy on Mother's face as my blood sprayed the wall, I spotted one of the poets who had recited on Bad Poetry Night. It was Mary Contrary, the adorable little waif whose eyes had inspired me to write my very own terrible poem. One of the effects of gin is that it can cause a person to stare inappropriately at something desirable for far longer than should be considered anywhere near 'cute' or 'harmless' and veer off into 'rohypnol' or 'disturbing' territory. Mary noticed my eyes searching for a glimpse of hers and she gave a snicker and turned away, back to the conversation she was having with a group of dapper young folks who seemed to be able to hold their liquor. They had one up on me.

It was entirely to my benefit that evening that I was both an obsessive and a coward, because my drunken lout of a self decided to head home and hit the laundry rather than making a fool of myself and it got me thinking. The walk home was filled with thoughts about what kind of a woman would want to be with a guy like me? I imagined inviting her over to have a romp on some old shirts and maybe literally roll out of bed into the kitchen to make some breakfast. I made up my drunken mind right there and then that I would get myself together and, once satisfied that I could have another human being share space with me in that apartment, I would ask Mary Contrary to come over for coffee.

This meant that I would have to buy a coffee maker.

And another mug.

And that meant being far less useless.

The thought of being less useless gave my drunken head an idea. After giving the area surrounding the lock on my apartment door a good awkward scratching with my fumbled keys, I tumbled into the boxes and dug out my most recent writing binder. Squinting at the pages I found the one that was needed, the one which I had created during my time at Dirk's and which we had posted up over town. The one in which I had tortured the word 'USEFUL' and surrounded it with crocodiles. I had formulated a tipsy idea. Realizing that there were not yet any magnets on my empty fridge, my lubricated hands smoothed out the paper on the small counter and I tumbled into my laundry bed, pulled a sweater over myself to keep warm and passed out.

In the morning, my mind snapped awake and miraculously remembered the goal that had been set out the night before. Happy to realize that today was not a work day, I set out to shop.

The first stop had been to a little furniture store. An oily clerk approached and proceeded to try and sell me on the giant leather couch I had sat upon to rest while a decision was made.

"I see you have fine taste in a sofa," the man began. "This one here is the most comfortable we have in stock, the back is made from a single animal, not a seam on it. Comes in three colours, but black is the discerning customer's prime choice."

Standing with a smirk I replied, "Actually I was looking for something in a futon."

The man's face sank like stone revealing a disturbing elasticity that no doubt helped with all of those pretend smiles. "Well, we don't have much in the way of futons. They've fallen out a fashion a bit, but what we do have is over this way." He did seem to perk up a bit at the prospect of making any sale at all as he slithered away, motioning for me to follow him to the futons.

They did indeed have light stock: only three futons were out on display and of those, only one was in my entirely modest price range. The man made a valiant effort to sell me on the more expensive of the three, but the cheapest was the only one I was interested in.

"The price may be good, but the comfort level is not nearly as quality. The difference is quite noticeable," he said, pushing on the cheap one with an open palm, demonstrating the lack of spring in the mattress.

"That may be, but how would it compare to a pile of clothing?"

"A pile of... well, I'm sure it's better than a lumpy pile, but..."

"Sold."

The entirely disappointed clerk rang me up along with a twenty-five dollar delivery fee for the next day (miraculously, they delivered on a Sunday) and it was off to stop number two.

During my day out, I had successfully obtained a garbage can, a cheap coffee maker, a frying pan, a decent quantity of groceries and a fridge magnet in the shape of a unicorn. The rest of the night I cleaned, disposing of my random garbage, storing my boxes in the tiny closet and making a small pot of coffee. Before partaking in my beverage, I pinned the sheet containing the tortured word 'USEFUL' to the fridge and ripped one of the crocodiles off of the page. My drunken plan was coming to fruition. Each day I managed to keep myself in check, one of the elements of torture on that piece of paper would be removed until all that remained was the word 'USEFUL'. Hopefully by that time, the word and I would be one and the same.

The next day, after the arrival of the futon that would be both my bed and my couch, I set out with the memory card full of photos from my trip with Dirk, selected my few favourites and had them printed out at the local photo-mart. I snagged a few frames and a package of tacks as well and left for home to hang up some photos and make my home a little more homey.

On the way out, I noticed the pet store nearby the photo-mart and realized that in order to succeed in my plans, I would have to buy a fish and not kill it. The death of my poor nameless friend must be avenged!

And so, there I was, plastic bag full of photos in hand, and a store full of fearful fish.

The fighting fish in their little glasses all looked very content and borderline lethargic. A wave of realization came over me.

"I had one of these!" A giddy smile plastered on my face, I pointed at one that looked almost identical to the one that had died on me just over a month ago.

"How did you like it?" the clerk asked.

"It was a friend in my times of greatest need," I said. "It showed me the error of my ways and died for my sins."

The clerk took a step back, perhaps instinctively stepping away from a man who may or may not be a little unstable. Excitedly, I pointed again at my poor dead fish's doppelgänger and declared: "I'll take it! Er... him. Or her. Whatever."

The clerk obliged and once our transaction was complete, I left with a brand new fishbowl and a moderately priced new friend. And some food. This one would actually get some food.

After setting out a space on the counter with the new bowl prepped and ready with water, I transferred my little fish into his new home and gave him the once over.

He had the same red in his fins as the one previous, but seemed so much livelier, flitting about his bowl in zigs and zags, testing out his new digs. With a few gentle taps, a flurry of fish food flakes fell down into the bowl and he gobbled at them with gusto, head held high, chin up, mouth sucking back the delicious wafer thin treats.

He needed a good professional sounding name, something with panache and gusto.

"Doctor Richard Ferguson." I said out loud. "You shall henceforth be called, Doctor Richard Ferguson."

With that, I carefully tore one of the crocodiles from the page on my fridge, pulled out my futon, placed a sweater over me for warmth and slept with a smile on my face.

Twenty-Two

Grave Danger

"HE THINKS YOU'RE SELFISH. Did you know that?"
I stood over Derrick Danger's grave with a bouquet of white lilies. My Grandmother had told me once that these were appropriate flowers for death. This had been discovered by accident when, as a child, I had chosen white lilies as a gift for her birthday. My Mother had thought nothing of it, other than that the flowers looked pretty, and the look of disgust on my Grandmother's face had been something of a disappointment to us both.

"You probably already know that."

I sat down, folded my legs beneath me and picked a blade of grass to chew on as I had seen Dirk do when we had come here together.

"He helped me out, your brother. I don't even know what I'm doing here..."

My teeth separated the milky root of the grass from the green leaf and a thin sweetness slid over my tongue.

"Dirk said your parents had been too hard on you. I understand that. My parents were never easy on me... You know, when I was a kid, I wanted to be a palaeontologist, go out and dig up Dinosaurs. I had all of these books and toys and a little fossil of a trilobite from the Tyrrell Musem. That place is kid heaven, I swear. My parents kind of sloughed it off as a fad or something and I remember this one time my Father told me, 'You're wasting your time with those Dinos kid. When you grow up there won't be anything left to dig up. They'll all be found by then.' That statement affected me in the weirdest way. Since he was Dad, surely he must be right. Grown-ups have all the answers, don't they? So, I started applying this logic to everything, thinking that there must be so much that will no longer be around when I was an adult. Once when the Olympics were on TV, in this moment of awkward childhood sexuality, I found myself smitten with a figure skater in her ridiculous, gaudy, sequined uniform and I thought, 'The pretty girls will all be gone by the time I grow up too.' The future would have no Dinosaurs and no pretty girls."

Laughing, I plucked another piece of grass to introduce my teeth to as my fingers tightened on the shiny wrapping that encased the lilies.

"That's kind of funny, but things were much worse, with the divorce and all. At least your parents were together! Fucker. You go and off yourself because your parents expect too much from you. You know, my parents fought and fought even after the divorce, but I sucked it up. What did you do?"

My hand had tightened in a fist around the lilies. Realizing the grip was breaking the stems inside, I threw them down at the foot of the grave, wondering briefly if that counted as littering.

"My parents," I continued, "were never supportive, only interested in themselves and constantly made bad decisions. My Father lives in hiding and my Mother can't find the time to be a Mother in between jobs and boyfriends. I wish my parents were as supportive as yours were. Sure they pushed you too hard, but so what? So fucking what?"

A lump caught in my throat, tears welling somewhere behind my eyes. All of this felt wrong. There was no reason that I should be here. I came to find some kind of closure, still wanting to know Dirk in some capacity, to thank him again for this help. This slab of rock with a rotting corpse beneath it was just another potential meeting spot, a place where Danger might appear and take me for a coffee. Things were all right at home. I was nearly 'USEFUL' for crying out loud, and yet something still seemed to be missing.

"Maybe I'm here to eulogize Dirk," I wondered aloud. "Maybe I'm saying goodbye to him by yelling at his dead brother."

A deep sigh slipped out, the first in a long time.

"He taught me quite a bit, you know. When we met I was a wreck. There were things we never really talked about. Things about me that just never came up. I dropped out of college. After turning eighteen, there was no way my Mother's house would continue to be my home, and I took this job as a tree planter of all things. I just wanted to get away, get anywhere far from my frightening little family and head for the hills. Didn't really cut it as a tree planter; never got the hang of any of it, and the job was lost after about a month. It was in the middle of nowhere, in northern BC and there I was, fired with a paycheque for about a thousand dollars and nowhere to go; nowhere to *be*, even. It was pretty exciting and there were all of these ideas swirling though my head about college and making a name for myself. There would be a degree in English attained and I would write stories.

"Instead of going somewhere far, far away from my family, I moved back to the same city I had fled, found a cheap room for rent and enrolled in school. The tree planting money dried up pretty quick and since I couldn't hold a job, I wasn't able to pay for my schooling and that was that. No more school. And then for five fucking years I played adult and failed miserably until Dirk came along and saved me from squalor. He's a good guy. He's doing all that he does in your memory, trying to make a difference so that more people don't end up like you. He never came out and said it, but you and I both know that's the way it is."

A thought occurred to me. Another mini epiphany flickered into focus. The best way to eulogize Dirk would be to carry on doing what he was doing in some capacity or another. I had to find some way to help others and maybe I could find my closure.

"I've got the answer, you magnificent bastard!" I yelled. "You will not have the last laugh. I haven't failed yet!"

Realizing that I had been yelling and spinning in a circle, suddenly on my feet and appearing to be dancing on Derrick's grave, I stopped cold.

"I'm yelling at a dead person in a cemetery..."

The words left my mouth with a certain realization. Derrick Danger wasn't a person I had any right to yell at. Derrick Danger was nothing more than a pigeon that won't eat and keeps pecking at its own reflection and I was just a confused little man yelling at himself.

Twenty-Three

Pressing On and On and On

"M-O-P-E" SHE SAID. "WE should go with Mope."
Things were interesting and we were
attempting to keep them that way.

After weeks of keeping myself afloat and drinking a little
too often at Dave's, my nerve had finally collected to the point
where I was able to speak to the lovely Miss Mary Contrary.
She was at the artillery and bakery joint almost every night,
and whenever I saw her, my eyes always felt the need to linger
a little too long. All right, I lied. I never had the nerve to talk
to her. She came up to me.

It went a little like this:

MARY — Hey!

ME — Oh... uh, hello.

MARY — Are your eyes all right?

ME — Yes... no?

MARY — Good gin?

ME — Very.

MARY — I ask if your eyes are all right because I seem to
find you looking over at me with this squint.

ME — This squint? (Here, I performed the squint, a mixture of 'I've had too much to drink' and 'what's that over there?')

MARY — Yeah, that's the one.

ME — Oh, no, it's not a squint.

MARY — What is it then? A leer?

ME — More of an ogle.

(Somehow here, she giggled, which was hopefully not a sympathy-for-the-drunk-and-infirm kind of giggle)

MARY — Are you always this forward?

ME — I rather quite backward.

MARY — I see.

ME — I'm sorry if I offended you...

MARY — You didn't. Don't worry about it.

ME — Well then I take it back.

MARY — Okay...

ME — So, you come here often?

(Incredibly, another giggle)

MARY — I'm sure that you're aware that I do. I see you over here every night, by yourself, squint-ogling over in my direction.

ME — Well, just look at that guy! (I pointed to one of the young men she had been standing with.) He's pretty...

MARY — Flashy? Neato?

ME — No, just pretty.

(Another giggle!)

MARY — You care to join us?

ME — This is surely an interesting night. Yes, I will join you.

And with that, I had a great and drunken time with honest to goodness people. It turned out that Mary's real name was Iris. We broke away from the group after a while and in my sotted way, I explained where I had first seen her and under what circumstances. She had remembered my poem and her wonderful eyes lit up when I told her that she had inspired it in all its awfulness. The conversation turned to Dirk and we talked all about his lessons and what had transpired. She was particularly fascinated with the 'keeping it interesting' mantra and the flipper story. After more fantastic conversation, we decided that we would meet again, outside of the café and do something ridiculous.

We became fairly regular companions, with our initial get together involving hiding little notes in books all throughout the local library. It was her idea and she had come with some notes prepared and a stack of blank paper and a marker to make more together. The notes read things like 'The lactose intolerant pledge that this book presents a negative reflection of their affliction' or 'Despite what you may have read, this book was well received among midgets, who prefer to be called "little people"'. We chose the books at random and shoved in our notes, trying to be as haphazard as possible. After finishing off with the notes we headed back to 'Dave's' for a celebratory gin or two.

Despite the fact that we had begun to hang out together quite frequently, it did become apparent to me that this was a very one sided relationship as far as the love interest went.

One night, after polishing off some imbibements, we staggered back to my place and after speaking at great length on the glories of Dr. Richard Ferguson, we fell into a kiss and then another and another. Being that we were quite tipsy, we passed out in a bit of a snuggle and when I awoke, she had left the apartment. There was a note stuck to my fridge that said 'Tonight, 7 o'clock, my place'.

Ecstatic, I showered far longer than necessary, grateful that water was included in the modest price of rent and prepared myself for what would surely be a night of delicious romance. Flowers would burst out of my eyes, rainbows would leak out of my skull and cute puppies would tear off all of my skin. Pure rapture.

Smelling like a pine tree and wearing my best tie, I arrived at the appointed hour to find that we were not in fact to entangle ourselves in delight, but would instead be watching a film with her friend Jason. A romantic comedy that we were not at all watching with a detached irony. The smell of my musky pine was commented on. It was an atrocity.

These mixed messages continued and would continue for as long as I deigned to put up with them. For some reason, I'm all right with this. I don't deserve a happy ending yet. I haven't earned it. The fact that someone wants to hang out with me on a regular basis and kiss me when she forgets herself is well and good enough for me.

Of course, I love the torment.

On this particular day, we were sitting and looking at my phone number, determining what words could be created using the last 4 digits. We had planned on setting up my answering machine to pick up with a message based on what we came up with.

It seemed that Iris had settled on 'Mope'.

'Mope it is," I replied.

We settled on a message for our fliers:

FEELING BLUE?

NEED A PICK-ME-UP?

SUCK AT LIFE?

CALL 555-MOPE

The answering machine message would play 'Don't Worry Be Happy'. If someone left a message, we'd cross that bridge when we came to it.

Collecting our fliers, we hit the town.

The night before, I had snipped off the last part of my 'word picture' and was officially 'USEFUL'. It was a momentous occasion, punctuated with me picking up Dr. Richard Ferguson's fishbowl and placing a greasy kiss against the glass. He pecked at the other side of the glass after the bowl had been set down and I'd like to think we shared a bit of a moment.

There was never any explanation given Iris as to what the bizarre jumble of sliced paper was stuck to the fridge, but she had noticed it shrinking. When she asked, I said something cryptic like 'Only time will tell' and she let it be.

I had been writing so much more as well. After the visit to Derek's grave, I had renewed vigour and decided that just as Dirk had worked in the memory of his brother, I would work in memory of Dirk. I hadn't been keeping a journal at all during the stay with Danger, but began to write mildly exaggerated accounts of what had transpired between us with the hope that in my own way, I might be reaching out to some reader the way that Dirk had reached out to me.

As I watched Iris reaching up with her insanely attractive arms (apparently, arms can be quite fetching), I saw her as a culmination of my tribulations. She was a symbol that I could have friends, I could be clean enough to have people visit me and I could potentially, and far into the future, find someone to love. Which is officially cheesy, but hey, they don't call me Cheesebomb for nothing.

Taping up those posters made me feel good, like I was making my presence felt and making people's lives just a little different. Certainly not better, but different. There will always be shit to overcome, but that's just life. Dirk wasn't perfect at it, my parents sure as hell aren't perfect at it and I will never be perfect at it. But I can try.

Plus, I wrote this book, and if you're reading it, I guess I'm not forgotten or too much of a failure after all.

I guess there's nothing really left to say but, "I was here."

About the Author

CHRIS ROTHE IS A cat and pun enthusiast living in Calgary with his calico Majig. His two biggest dreams are:

1. That you enjoy this book and any other materials that he shall produce
2. That he will one day create a hoax that is told back to him years later as a factual statement.

If you see him on the street, he will gladly buy you a coffee and discuss any manner of pretentious things.

Here's some we
made earlier...

THE BEAUTIFUL RED

A collection by **JAMES COOPER**

Forward by **CHRISTOPHER FOWLER**

Red...

The colour that surrounds us as we enter the world;
the colour that consumes us when we die.

Red...

The colour of life and everything in it.

Red...

The colour we produce when we scream...

The Beautiful Red

12 extraordinary tales of madness and dysfunction, dissecting the
red world, where only the sound of our violence can be heard...

A brand-new collection of twelve horror tales from **James Cooper**.
This, his second collection, comes complete with a foreword
from the Award-Winning Master of Urban Horror: **Christopher
Fowler.**

The quality of [James Cooper's] *output so far easily matches
that of the best-known talents in contemporary horror.*

— **Carl Hays**; *Booklist*

*It's been quite a while since I've encountered stories like this,
tales that ignore topical tastes in favour of a strange view
of humanity that's timeless, classical, and mysteriously sad.*

— **Christopher Fowler** (from his foreword)

[James Cooper is] *one of the most promising writers to
emerge from the small press pack in recent years.*

— **Peter Tennant**; *Black Static*

Paperback: $19⁹⁹/£11⁹⁹ ‡ ISBN: 978-0-9811597-0-6
E-Book: $9⁹⁹/£4⁹⁹ ‡ ISBN: 978-0-9811597-6-8

WICKED DELIGHTS

A collection by **JOHN LLEWELLYN PROBERT**

Wicked...

The book that sucks the blood from children

... Delights

The film that turns people into self-destructive
sadomasochistic obsessives

Wicked...

The lunatic asylum that steals souls

... Delights

The art exhibition of mutilated humanity...
where the exhibits are still alive!

John Llewellyn Probert's latest short story collection – containing eighteen delicious selections across 352 delectable pages – mixes the cruel with the carnal, the sadistic with the sexual, the erotic with the outrageous, to bring you tales of a cuckolded husband's terrible revenge, the television channel where you can pay off your debts but at the worst price imaginable, the man willing to do anything to improve his chances of success with the ladies, a marriage guidance counsellor who goes to bloody extremes to prove her point, the woman who will do anything to keep her family, and a city made entirely from human bone. All of this, and the last Christmas ever, just to make things even *more* cheery.

★ *Vividly creepy images... are all the more compelling when rendered in Probert's breezy style.*

— *Publishers Weekly*

There's dark humour here, and unexpected poignancy — indeed, the book is as full of surprises as the man himself. Horror is lucky to have him.

— **Ramsey Campbell**

Jacket-less Hardback: $39⁹⁹/£22⁹⁹   ‡   ISBN: 978–0–9811597–2–0
E-Book: $9⁹⁹/£4⁹⁹   ‡   ISBN: 978–0–9811597–7–5

TWISTHORN BELLOW
A novel by RHYS HUGHES

Rhys Hughes once again foists his mad tale-spinning ability upon the world with this brand-new novel of monsters attacking all that is bad (musicians, Frenchmen... you know, *those* sort of people), tipping his hat in the direction of both '**Hellboy**' and **Philip José Farmer** in the process. when this author describes something as "this is the maddest thing I've ever written", you know you're in for something special.

It may come as no surprise that France wants to take over the world again. But this time they plan to go much further and gain control of the spiritual dimensions too, making French the official language of the afterlife! Twisthorn Bellow is a freshly baked golem who has fallen into a vat of nitroglycerin, turning him into a living stick of dynamite. As well as battling against monsters and rock musicians, he's the only thing that can preserve and protect the glorious British Empire and prevent the French-ification of the entire cosmos. But considering the French have all the best ideas and tunes, he doesn't stand a soufflé in Hell's chance!

Few living fictioneers approach this chef's sardonic confections, certainly not in English.
— **Michael Moorcock**

Rhys Hughes is more fun than one of those barrels of monkeys people talk about, and you're probably going to have a good time with his book.
— **Peter Tennant**; *Black Static*

Just beginning to read: saliva already forming on chin.
— **Brian Aldiss**

Paperback: 19^{99}/£11^{99} ‡ ISBN: 978−0−9811597−1−3
E-Book: 9^{99}/£4^{99} ‡ ISBN: 978−0−9811597−5−1

THE TERROR AND THE TORTOISESHELL
A novel by JOHN TRAVIS

John Travis's first novel, *The Terror and the Tortoiseshell*, is a *noir*–styled murder mystery with deft touches of both the Comedy and Science Fiction genres, but primary in it is the honouring of the classic hard-boiled detective novels of the 1940s.

Benji Spriteman takes over the "Spriteman Detective Agency" after the world is changed overnight by 'The Terror', resulting in the animal kingdom moving from four legs to two and banishing the now crazy human population from existence to become the dominant species. Oh, and Benji Spriteman is a sentient, six-foot tall, suit-wearing, Tortoiseshell cat. Yeah, that's a bit of a jolt, especially to Benji.

In this strange environment, which sees animals taking on some of the characteristics of the humans they were closest to, human beings have become a bit like flying saucers – despite occasional sightings, there is never any definite proof that they still exist. But when humans do start to appear it's always in the most bizarre situations – always dead, and 'displayed' as if they were animals. And it's just as Benji's life is starting to become a bit more 'normal' that he gets drawn into the investigation into these murders, and soon finds himself involved in ways he could never have imagined...

John Travis is a madcap cross between Monty Python and Clive Barker. His stories percolate like a popcorn machine full of jungle beetles!

— **Mark Mclaughlin**

★ Animal Farm *meets* The Big Sleep*... compelling hard-boiled mystery... superior work... fully realized imaginary world.*
— ***Publishers Weekly***

Jacket-less Hardback: $34⁹⁹/£19⁹⁹   ‡   ISBN: 978–0–9811597–3–7
E-Book: $9⁹⁹/£4⁹⁹   ‡   ISBN: 978–0–9811597–4–4

ATOMIC FEZ PUBLISHING

Eclectic, Genre-Busting Fiction

www.AtomicFez.com